John A. Hall

The Great Strike on the Q

John A. Hall

The Great Strike on the Q

ISBN/EAN: 9783337366933

Printed in Europe, USA, Canada, Australia, Japan

Cover: Foto ©Andreas Hilbeck / pixelio.de

More available books at **www.hansebooks.com**

GREAT STRIKE ON THE "Q"

WITH

A HISTORY OF THE ORGANIZATION AND GROWTH OF THE
BROTHERHOOD OF LOCOMOTIVE ENGINEERS, BROTHER-
HOOD OF LOCOMOTIVE FIREMEN, AND SWITCH-
MEN'S MUTUAL AID ASSOCIATION
OF NORTH AMERICA.

BY

John A. Hall,

Ex-Yardmaster C. B. & Q. Railway.

———

1889.
ELLIOTT & BEEZLEY,
CHICAGO AND PHILADELPHIA.

DEDICATION.

A history of the spoliations, robberies, and oppressions of corporate capital in America, is a history of shame, degredation and disgrace, not to be obscured in the halo of great achievements in material progress, though adorned by the splendid triumphs of science and art. It is the impersonation of the passion of avarice, and no more soul-debasing passion afflicts the human race. It becomes more ravenous the more its maw is gorged; it always and everlastingly wants more; in growth it never reaches maturity.

The only firm and determined resistance that has ever confronted this power has come from the widely extended but fraternally combined labor organizations of the country; though not always successful in resistance, they have ever left the enemy too feeble to follow up a technical victory.

To that mighty bulwark that will yet stem the tide of corporate greed, and insure to the laborer a fair share of the produce of his toils, this book is respectfully dedicated.

PREFACE.

THE cause of right is but the cause of reason. Let all men reason together, and be brothers. Let all help each other and it will be easier for all.

We are all victims of monopoly, and it lies within our own efforts to reform a system which enslaves the many and makes heartless misers of the few. We must not fear a thing because it seems radical; truth is always radical, and every advance that humanity has ever made has been born in radicalism.

To act upon the dictates of reason is to be radical. This fearful thing called radicalism is the hope of society. With it you will bury monopoly, injustice and oppression.

Him the world calls Master, because of His worthiness, nobleness, manhood and justice, was far from being conservative. He espoused the cause of the poor, the weak and the helpless against the rich, the strong, and the powerful. Instead of favoring and fostering the existing evils of society, He sought to reform them, and set into motion the great wheels of Christianity that are rolling over the whole earth. Let those who call themselves His followers, strive to make His commands practicable. Let them have more of justice, charity and humanity.

ORGANIZATION.

To obtain justice, and obtain it legally, the weak must organize. Whatever may be the ideal to which labor reformers aspire, the first step must be organization. This is living protest against monopoly and injustice, and the means by which we must reform our social system, if we would last as a nation.

A tramp at the base of the social pyramid, and a millionaire at the top, argues ill for the middle classes. With the foundation rotten, and the summit top-heavy, the whole structure must fall or be rebuilt.

Much of the matter contained in this book came under the personal observation of the writer; more was furnished by the Brotherhoods and the correspondence of the strikers.

Thanks are due to Chairmen Hoge and Murphy, for kindness and favors rendered.

Yours Truly,

JOHN A. HALL.

THE GREAT STRIKE ON THE Q.

THIS work should properly begin with a short history of the origin and growth of the three Orders whose members were connected with the strike upon the Burlington system.

Naturally the Brotherhood of Locomotive Engineers should come first, as the strike originated with them, and was brought about by the injustice and oppression of the Burlington Officials toward this Order.

The organization of the Brotherhood of Locomotive Engineers originated in the State of Michigan, in the year 1863. For some years before that time, the locomotive engineers on various roads throughout the country had cause for serious complaints owing to the treatment they received at the hands of railroad officials. It was felt that the men handling the locomotives on the growing railroad system of America were performing important duties that required good, responsible men, and deserved fair and honorable treatment, which, in many instances, was not given. The tendency of many railroad officers, in fact, was to degrade engineers, and refuse them the justice and fair dealing which is their just due. The immediate cause of the formation of the Order was the harsh treatment received by the engineers employed on the Michigan Central Railroad from the superintendent of motive power of that road. The disposition manifested by him to wage a remorseless war upon the best interests of labor, and especially his incroachments upon the established rights and usages of the engineers in the employ of that company, and the reduction of their pay, at length became insufferable, and the engineers, as a class, became satisfied that the safety of their pecuniary interests demanded a unity of purpose and combined organization. A meeting was held, composed of engineers employed by the Michigan Central Railroad, and the result of their deliberations, at this primary meeting, was a call for a Convention of Engineers, to meet in the city of Detroit, on the fifth of the ensuing month, May. The call was extended only to the engineers on the following roads: The Michigan Central, Michigan Southern & Northern Indiana, Detroit & Milwaukee, Grand Trunk on the American side, and the Detroit Branch of the Michigan Southern. At the Convention, the Michigan Southern & Northern Indiana was represented by F. Avery, L. Wheeler and John Kennedy; the Detroit Branch of that road by T. Wartsmouth and E. Nichols; the Detroit & Milwaukee by H. Higgins; the Grand Trunk by B. Northrup; and Geo. Q. Adams represented the Eastern Division of the Michigan Central, and W. D. Robinson the Middle Division of the same road. With but little formality in their organization, these delegates entered upon their duties. A Constitution and By-Laws, embodying the fundamental principles of our present organization, was adopted.

The necessity of something further on the part of engineers than the common consent to become and remain members of this organization so long as suited their convenience, and no longer, became apparent to minds of the delegates, and an obligation, as a bond of union, was unanimously adopted, and on the 8th of May, 1863, a band of twelve engineers, the delegates included, joined hands and pledged themselves to support the Constitution and By-Laws then adopted, and to resist the wrong and maintain the right. Officers were elected, and Division No. 1, of Detroit, Brotherhood of the Foot-Board, stood forth as the pioneer in the work of the regeneration and elevation of the locomotive engineers on this continent, eager to extend the hand of fellowship and alliance to all worthy members of the craft who had any faith in their rights as a class and a belief that in organized action alone rested a hope of vindication. The organization of Divisions soon began, and in three months ten Divisions had sprung into existence.

At this time, the Chief Engineer of Division No. 1 issued a call for a meeting of one delegate from each Division, to meet at Detroit August 18, 1863, for the purpose of forming a Grand National Division, Brotherhood of Locomotive Engineers. At this meeting, the Constitution and By-Laws were changed and provisions made for the formation and government of a Grand National Division. W. D. Robinson was elected Grand Chief Engineer of the Order, and served in that capacity until August 20, 1864, at which time there were thirty-eight Sub-Divisions, covering the railroads from Michigan, through Indiana, Illinois, Ohio, Kentucky, Tennessee, Pennsylvania, New Jersey and New York. Charles Wilson, the second Grand Chief Engineer, was elected to succeed W. D. Robinson, and continued in office until February 25, 1874.

At a special session of the Grand International Division, held in the city of Cleveland, P. M. Arthur, the present incumbent, was elected his successor, and re elected at the close of each term of three years to the present time, executing the duties of the office with such success and judgment that the Order has continued to grow and improve, until it now numbers three hundred and sixty Sub-Divisions with 25,000 members, and covers every railroad and every State and Territory in the United States, as well as a large part of the British Provinces and Mexico. We believe that the law of the Order, enforced by him, of "doing by others as we would be done by," is the only true solution to the labor problem of the present day.

In these days of strikes and increasing labor agitation, the course adopted by them has proved to be unquestionably the best, and to that alone we ascribe the great success that has attended their efforts and made their Order known and respected everywhere. This course is, that any differences between members and their employers shall be settled by arbitration. St. Paul says, "Come, let us reason together;" and this advice they have found to be so good that they have it to say, that never since its adoption by them have they resorted to a strike when the officials of a company where dissatisfaction existed would receive and treat with our committee.

Brotherhood of Locomotive Firemen.

The organization known as the Brotherhood of Locomotive Firemen was organized at Port Jervis, N. Y., December 1, 1873, and is consequently fifteen years old.

The following "Preamble" to the Constitution explains the aims and objects of the Order:

For the purpose of uniting Locomotive Firemen, and elevating their social, moral and intellectual standing, and for the protection of their interests and the promotion of their general welfare, the Brotherhood of Locomotive Firemen has been organized.

The interests of our members and their employers being identical, we recognize the necessity of co-operation, and it is the aim of the Brotherhood to cultivate a spirit of harmony between them, upon a basis of mutual justice.

Realizing the fact that our vocation involves ceaseless peril, and that it is a duty we owe to ourselves and our families to make suitable provision against these disasters which almost daily overtake us on the rail, the necessity of protecting our interests as firemen and of extending to each other the hand of charity, and being sober, industrious and honorable men, becomes self-evident: And, hence, the Brotherhood has adopted as its cardinal principles, the motto: "Protection, Charity, Sobriety and Industry."

The organization was formed by eleven men on the Erie Railroad, and the first Lodge numbered eleven men. Its growth and development has been phenomenal; starting with that first Lodge of eleven men in New York, the organization expanded into immense proportions, with lodges in every State and Territory of the Union, covering Canada and extending into Mexico.

There are at present 385 subordinate lodges, with a membership of 19,000 men. The rapid growth fully demonstrates the necessity for its existence. It might be supposed that this phenomenal increase would be a source of weakness, instead of strength. Such, however, is not the case. The Brotherhood of Firemen has never, at anytime, been unwieldy, but on the contrary the addition of each new lodge has been so well assimulated by the whole, that this body of 19,000 is as compact, firm and as thoroughly under control as a division of the Regular Army. Another grand element of strength is the fact that there is no aristocracy in the Order.

It must not be thought that all has been clear and smooth sailing with the Brotherhood of Firemen; this great result has been won by years of incessant labor by earnest, determined men, with confidence in themselves and in the justice of their cause. Probably no organization has had a harder struggle for existence; it has experienced serious reverses; the year of its birth was the year of the great commercial panic. Born and nutured in adversity, it has steadily worked its way to the front. In 1877 the country was agitated from Maine to California by labor troubles, and labor organizations received a severe check, and an unsettled condition existed for several years.

"Seventy-eight" and "'79" were critical periods, and were years of anxiety for the safety of the Brotherhood.

Starting in 1873 as a purely benevolent institution, it developed into a labor organization in 1885, retaining, however, all of its moral and benevolent features intact. There are no State organizations in this Brotherhood. It is governed by a Grand Lodge composed of a Grand Master, Vice-Grand Master, Grand Secretary and Treasurer, Editor and Manager of the Magazine, Grand Executive Board of five members, and a Board of Grand Trustees, consisting of three members.

OFFICERS.

The first Grand Master was J. A. Leach, now residing in Kansas City; the first Grand Secretary and Treasurer was Wm. N. Sayre, of Buffalo, N. Y.; second Grand Master, W. R. Worth, followed in succession by F. B. Alley and W. T. Goundie (now General Manager of the New York Elevated Railway), and F. W. Arnold. S. M. Stevens, of Lowell, Mass., was, for several years, Grand Organizer and Instructor, succeeded in 1885 by J. J. Hannahan, of Englewood, Ill., who now holds that office in connection with that of Vice-Grand Master.

The present officers are: F. P. Sargent, Grand Master, Terre Haute, Ind.; J. J. Hannahan, Vice-Grand Master and Grand Organizer and Instructor, Englewood, Ill.; Eugene V. Debs, Grand Secretary and Treasurer, Terre Haute, Ind.; H. H. Walton is Chairman of the Grand Executive Board, Philadelphia, Pa.; W. E. Burns, Secretary, Chicago, Ill.; the Grand

Executive Board is composed of J. J. Leahy, Philadelphia, Pa.; W. H. McDonnell, Scranton, Pa.; F. Holl, Minneapolis, Minn., and C. W. Gardner, Fort Dodge, Ia.

The circulation of the Magazine, the official organ of the Brotherhood is 26,000 copies.

BENEVOLENCE OUTSIDE OF THE ORDER.

Standing squarely on the broad principles of Benevolence and Human Justice, this Order has ever extended the helping hand and given counsel and assistance to the laboring man in his struggle for independence. The Brotherhood of Railway Brakemen owe much to the B. of L. F., and never in its history has the B. of L. F. opposed itself to labor organization. Remembering their own desperate struggle for existence, charity, sympathy and aid have been freely given to younger organizations.

Ever foremost in the battle for justice and right, it was the first to call attention to the imperative necessity for federation of railroad employes. The strike upon the "Q" has demonstrated the absolute need of federation.

GRAND MASTER SARGENT.

The following extract from the address of Grand Master Sargent, at Minneapolis, three years ago, covers many of the points in controversy to-day, and will be found interesting to the public:

The Brotherhood of Locomotive Firemen ask nothing that is not just; we do not want one penny more than we rightfully earn; we believe that our calling is one that should command good wages for faithful service, and we desire also that all our members shall render such service. We recognize the fact that our employer has certain rights that we, as employes, are bound to respect, and it is never our purpose to antagonize. Justice is our motto—justice not only to ourselves, but to our employer. I believe that if organizations of labor keep in mind that great principle, and are officered by men that are conservative, that are willing to work at both sides of a question and settle on a basis of equal justice to both employer and employe, and when the employer will be willing to treat his employe with that spirit of fairness which is due all faithful workmen, recognizing in them men of intelligence, capable of knowing right from wrong, that strikes and strife will seldom come, and if they do, it will be when every well-thinking man that has the true principle of manhood will endorse the organization struggling for its rights. I desire the members of the Brotherhood of Locomotive Firemen to so conduct themselves that when they go before a General Manager, Superintendent or Master Mechanic, they will meet with those courtesies due a manly man. I want General Managers, Superintendents and Master Mechanics to feel that they have in a member of the Brotherhood of Locomotive Firemen a faithful employe, one they can place confidence in, and when he comes to them in a respectful way, and lays before them a grievance, that they will give him a hearing and render him justice.

Our system of adjusting grievances is by arbitration, believing this is the only sure method of preserving harmony between employer and employe. If at any time we feel aggrieved, we make a statement of our grievance and place it in the hands of the Grievance Committee of the local Lodge. The chairman of this committee, through its secretary, calls the committee together, and examines into the merits of the grievance, and if considered just, the committee so reports to the Lodge with proper recommendations, and if the Lodge considers the grievance worthy of action, it orders the committee to proceed to adjust the matter. The committee then calls on the Master Mechanic and Superintendent, and in a gentlemanly manner lay the grievance before them, and if possible arrive at a satisfactory settlement. If the Master Mechanic and Superintendent have not the power, or show

2

no disposition to treat with the committee, they go to the General Manager, from him to the President, and so on until all means have been exhausted to secure an adjustment. If they fail, they then send for their chief executive, and on his arrival, he, in conjunction with the committee, again uses all means within reason to effect a settlement. Failing again, it then lies in the power of the Grand Master to order the men to quit work, or, in more plain terms, to strike. Now, the Brotherhood of Locomotive Firemen have been in existence nearly thirteen years, and during that time we have not been involved in a single strike. We believe that the conservative stand that has always been taken, and the intelligence of the men that have been our leaders and committees have been the means of making this record. It has been said that firemen would never be recognized by railway officials in the adjustment of wages or the settlement of grievances. I desire to dispel any such opinion from the minds of all. During the last year we have had a large number of our committees wait on Presidents and General Managers, and in every instance they were cordially treated and received a satisfactory advance of pay, and the result is that firemen are looked upon by officials as men capable of reasoning, that they are qualified to go before a President or General Manager and discuss questions relative to their vocation better than men that are not following the same occupation, even though they ride upon the same engine.

The Brotherhood feels proud of its record, and it is our purpose to carry forward our good work in the same straightforward manner. We ask nothing of our employer but what is reasonable, believing that it is the policy of the railway managers of the present day to treat with their employes in a fair and liberal manner. It has been my experience, during the limited time that I have been connected with railroads, that most of the dissatisfaction that arises between employer and employe originates from the overbearing, tyrannical action of some petty foreman, ofttimes a Master Mechanic, and employes censure the officials, and sometimes affairs assume a serious aspect, when, if the employe would go to the proper authority—the President or General Manager—and lay his grievance before them, he would get immediate satisfaction. Ofttimes the officials know nothing of the existence of any dissatisfaction until they are informed that the employe has struck; then it is too late to present the true situation to the official, who, having had no intimation of trouble, feels greatly incensed at the action of the employe, and immediately turns against him, when, had the facts been presented to him, the foreman or the petty boss that caused the dissatisfaction would have been looking for employment, while the employe would have had justice. There is only one way to adjust our grievances, and that. is by a careful statement to the proper authority. Then, if we fail to obtain satisfaction, we can feel that we have done our duty, and the responsibility rests with employer, not employe. During the past few months we have observed in many localities troubles between employer and employe. The cry has always been, Labor fighting capital. Capital is not the enemy of labor; it is not capital that labor is opposing; it is the monopolist, and such a monopolist grinds down the laboring man to starvation wages in order that he may enrich his own coffers. Labor is the creator of capital, and as such there can be no strife between them. It is the monopolists that control capital that antagonizes the laborer, and compels him to work for scarcely enough to keep his family in food; and it is those monopolists that to-day have capital bound in chains and separated from its creator—labor. For years laboring men have been subject to reductions in wages until, in many instances, the amount of their daily earnings would scarcely buy food sufficient to sustain life. Men of liberal views have observed this state of affairs, and many of our great thinkers have examined into this question, and, becoming convinced that it was wrong to allow their fellow-men to be trodden down by a class of men that have only one ambition, and that is to control all the capital of the land, have organized for the purpose of getting for the laborer, the creator of the vast wealth of this country, a reasonable day's pay for a reasonable day's work; not to antagonize capital, but to ask that he who creates the wealth of the land shall have at least enough to clothe and feed his family and live in a respectable little home. To be sure, there have many things occurred during the past few months that have caused some of these organizations of labor to be looked upon with suspicion, and there are many that stand ready to condemn them. But let us not be too severe;

we have all made mistakes. and we should always be willing
to concede to others what we ask for ourselves—charity ; and
let us be charitable to those that during the past year have
been involved in difficulties with their employers.

The members are not to be censured for all that is done
by these organizations. Officers that wield the power can
involve an Order in difficulty by making unjust demands.
Men ought never to be placed at the head of these labor organizations who are unprincipled or unjust. Place men there
who will work to the interests of those they represent, and at
all times avoid conflict when it is uncalled for. I am convinced that the labor troubles of the past few months have
been beneficial to us all, notwithstanding there have been
many wrongs committed, many lives lost and much property
destroyed.   This we all deplore, and any Order that sanctions
any such actions on the part of its members should be con-
demned. We believe that the trouble we have experienced will
teach a lesson to all organizations of labor. We cannot be
too careful whom we admit to our Order, one bad man may
ruin a whole Lodge. Look well to a man's character and
standing before you admit him. and then you will find that in
all his duties he will do right and bring credit to himself and
the Order. In admitting only such men, we may hope to receive the endorsement of all good people.

We turn to our Constitution, and there read in the preamb-
ble: "For the purpose of effecting a unity of Firemen, and
elevating them to a higher social, moral and intellectual
standard, and for the promotion of their general welfare, and
the protection of their families, the Brotherhood has been
organized."

Let these words be engraven upon the hearts, not only
of our membership, but the great public, so that our aims
may be understood and our ambitions appreciated. Our
preamble voices the sublime sentiments of our fraternity, and
we trust they may touch a responsive chord in the hearts of
all good people.

Switchmen's Mutual Aid Association of North America.

This Association is growing rapidly in influence and numbers. It is now one of the most powerful labor organizations on this continent. The large field from which it draws its membership, the character of its members, and the care exercised in admitting none but the right type of men, the energy and determination of each individual, and, above all other considerations, the absolute equality guaranteed by its Constitution and unwritten laws, warrant the assertion that this Association must soon stand among the first in the list of labor organizations.

OBJECT.

The preamble to the Constitution reads as follows:

1st. Is to unite and promote the general welfare and advance the interests, social, moral and intellectual, of its members. Benevolence, very needful in a calling as hazardous as ours, has led to the organization of this Association.

2d. Believing that it is for the best interests, both of our members and their employers, that a good understanding should at all times exist between them, it will be the constant endeavor of this Association to establish mutual confidence and create and maintain harmonious relations between employer and employe.

3d. Such are the aims and purposes of the Switchmen's Mutual Aid Association of North America.

Benevolence is its corner-stone,—to relieve the distress of disabled brothers, to care for their widows and orphans, and to see to the decent burial of deceased members.

The National Association, strong as it is in numbers, is but little over three years old.

The first Switchmen's Union was founded in Chicago, on August 18, 1877. That was a local society, and was chartered by the State of Illinois. The charter members were—Edward W. Jennings, Thos. Griffin, James Cullerton, Wm. Hopper, Thaddeus Boyd, Thos. Green, Edward Scanlon, John Kenny, Wm. Short, Chas. Richardson, Wm. Rosencranse and John Reily. The officers were—Wm. Hopper, President; Thaddeus Boyd, Vice-President; Thos. Griffin, James Cullerton and Edward Jennings, Trustees.

While for several years the Union made little headway, it succeeded in maintaining a nucleus for something better. In 1884, new life was instilled into it by the demands and spirit of the times, coupled with the selection of a set of officers with unusual energy, ability and determination. Rapid growth, and the creation and dissemination of sentiments of organization were the immediate results. Other cities followed Chicago's example, and very soon there were a number of flourishing Unions throughout the United States.

Then the necessity of a National organization became manifest. Several Unions, moved by the same spirit, took hold of this matter about the same time. A call for a meeting of delegates of the various local bodies, to meet at 112 East Randolph street, Chicago, on February 22, 1886, was issued, and in response thereto a large assemblage of representative switchmen met at the place on the day named. The meeting lasted eight days, and was quite harmonious and exceedingly enthusiastic. The Convention was called to order by Mr. John Drury, who stated that the object was to amalgamate the different organizations into one grand body, whose authority should extend throughout the United States. The Convention was duly organized by the election of Mr. John Drury as Chairman, Mr. James A. Healey, of Chicago, as Secretary, Mr. Joseph D. Hill, of Kansas City, Reading Clerk, and Mr. M. J. Keegan, Sergeant-at-Arms. A Constitution and By-Laws were adopted, and the following grand officers elected for the current year: Grand Master, James L. Monaghan; Vice-Grand Master and Instructor, John Drury; Grand Secretary and Treasurer, John Downey. Board of Directors, M. J. Keegan, of Chicago; James A. Kelly, of Chicago; W. A. Simmons, of Chicago; James A. Healey, of Chicago; Joseph D. Hill, of Kansas City; J. L. Hyer, of Rock Island, and W. R. Davison, of Joliet. A great deal of important business was transacted in secret session pertaining to the Order, after which the Grand Lodge resolved to aid Mr. C. R. Wooldridge in the publication of a monthly magazine devoted to the interests of the Order. A uniform pin was adopted, and an invitation to attend the second annual ball, given by local Lodge No. 1, in honor of the Grand Lodge, was accepted with thanks. The Convention then adjourned, to meet in Kansas City, Monday, September 20, 1886.

James L. Monaghan, the first Grand Master, graduated from the public schools of Philadelphia, and studied law for two years. Bad health, however, compelled him to abandon an indoor life, and he took to railroading. He first did duty as a clerk, but found that was little better for him than the law, and he then entered the service as a switchman on the P., W. & B. Ry. He came West in 1879, and has been prominently identified with the switchmen and their organizations until November, 1888, when he was elected to the lower house of the Illinois Legislature. He was succeeded in the office by Frank Sweeney, of Minneapolis.

John Drury, the first Vice-Grand Master, is an Englishman. He first entered upon railroad work as a brakeman on the Grand Trunk of Canada. As an organizer during the early days, John Drury was eminently successful, and the Association progressed in a surprising manner during the first year of its National existence. The First Annual Convention was held at Kansas City, September 20, 1886, and was composed of delegates from twenty-five Lodges. This represented the growth of the Order for one year.

The important business of the complete reconstruction of the Constitution and By-Laws to keep pace with the growing propensities of the Association, was the result of that body's deliberations.

The Second Annual Convention was held at Indianapolis, September 19, 1887. The result of this meeting was a still further revision of the laws, and the election of Wm. A. Simsrott as Grand Secretary and Treasurer.

At the Third Annual Convention at St. Louis, in September, 1888, Frank Sweeney, of Minneapolis, was elected Grand Master; John Downey, of Chicago, Vice-Grand Master; Geo. S. Bailey, Grand Organizer and Instructor. John W. Callahan, Chicago, Ill.; Edward Hutchinson, Chicago, Ill.; S. K. Hardin, St. Louis, Mo.; John M. Kelley, Fort Wayne, Ind.; Jas. F. Scullen, Omaha, Neb., Grand Board of Directors.

Grand Master Frank Sweeney was born in Zanesville, O., in 1855. His parents moved West in 1860, and located at Monroe, Wis. He received a common-school education, and for a time studied medicine. He disliked the profession, however, and soon abandoned it and entered the railway service. His first railroading was in the capacity of brakeman on the M. & St. P. After braking on several roads for the period of four years, he began switching in the yard of the Minneapolis & St. Louis in 1886. At that time there were but three switch engines in Minneapolis. He has been in the yard service in that city ever since, until elevated to the position of Grand Master of the Order. He was one of the active men that organized Lodge No. 30, and was elected a delegate to the Second Annual Convention, held in Indianapolis, in 1887. At that session he was elected Vice-Grand Master of the Association, and his recent elevation to the highest position in the Order speaks better than words as to what opinion the switchmen have of him. He was instrumental in organizing the Northwest, and

won the admiration of the switchmen of the country
by his intelligent and conservative handling of questions that arose in that locality.

Grand Secretary and Treasurer William A. Simsrott was born in Chicago in 1861, and has the hustle
characteristic of the average Chicagoan. He received
a common-school education, and began his railroading in 1878 as a clerk on the P., Ft. W. & C. Railway.   In 1882 he entered the yards of the Chicago
& Western Indiana Railway as a switchman.   In
1883 he entered the service of the L., N. A. & C.
Railway, and continued with that road until elected
to the office of Grand Secretary and Treasurer.   He
was a yardmaster at the time of leaving the company's employ.   He was accepted in Lodge No. 1 in
1883, and in a few months elected to the office of
Financial Secretary.   Mr. Simsrott was one of the
thirteen that established the Association as a National
organization, and was a delegate from Lodge No. 1 to
the First Annual Convention at Kansas City in 1886.
At this Convention he was chosen as one of the Grand
Board of Directors, and at the Second Annual Convention, held in Indianapolis in 1887, he was elected Grand
Secretary and Treasurer.   None have shown a higher
regard for the good of the Association than this officer.

Vice-Grand Master John Downey was born in
Cleveland, Ohio, October, 12, 1853, and came to Chicago in the fall of 1858.   He received a common
education, and in the winter of 1869–70 commenced
railroading.   He first began braking on the P., Ft.
W. & C. road, but soon went to switching in the Ft.

Wayne yards. He had not been there long, however, before he had his left thumb completely shot off by the accidental discharge of a shotgun he was handling. In September, 1871, he lost two fingers off of the right hand, after which he went to tending switches on the Ft. Wayne. In 1872 he had his right foot caught and lost part of it, and 1875 he had his left foot caught and so severely injured that it laid him up for six months. In 1876 he went braking on passenger on the Ft. Wayne, where he remained for nine months, when he went braking on freight, and 1879 went back switching in the Ft. Wayne yards, where he has remained ever since.

John Downey joined Lodge No. 1 in September, 1884, and was soon afterward elected Treasurer of the Lodge, a position he held continuously until October, 1887, when he resigned. He was elected Grand Secretary and Treasurer of the then Switchmen's Mutual Aid Association of the United States of America, at its first Convention, held in Chicago, February 22, 1886. He served for some time in this capacity, but was forced to resign, owing to ill health, and when W. S. Condon absconded with all the money of the Grand Lodge he was asked by the Board of Directors of the Grand Lodge to fill out the unexpired term as Grand Secretary and Treasurer, and straighten out the tangled financial affairs of the Grand Lodge. He responded with that patriotism he is noted for, and won encomiums from all connected with the Association for his work. He has represented Lodge No. 1

in the Grand Lodge twice—Kansas City in 1886 and St. Louis in 1888.

Grand Organizer and Instructor George S. Bailey was born in Edgar County, Illinois, in 1858. After receiving a common-school education, he studied law for some time, but had to abandon his studies on account of ill health. He commenced railroading in 1878 on the I. & St. L. Railway, braking on local freight. He was employed as a switchman in East St. Louis a number of years, and was prominent in the great railroad strike of 1886.

When the "Q" strike occurred, he was selected to go over a portion of the road and address the railroad men. He spoke at Kansas City, St. Joe, Council Bluffs and other western points. He was a delegate from Lodge No. 37 at the Convention of 1888, and was then elected to his present position. He was a member of the Illinois Legislature in 1886, and made a creditable record. He introduced, and had passed through the House, "House Bill No. 268," which provided for a State Board of Arbitration, but before it reached the Senate the General Assembly had adjourned. Mr. Bailey is full of energy and ability, yet does not allow his enthusiasm to overbalance his good judgment. He has the faculty of controlling men and at the same urging them on to a sense of the duty they owe to themselves and those dependent upon them, as well as to their employers.

It has been but a few months since the Convention of 1888, and already fifteen new Lodges have been organized, while about a dozen others are ready and are clamoring for admission to the Association. The whole Eastern section of the country yet remains to be organized, and the switchmen throughout that section are fully alive to the needs of the hour. The present year will witness the addition of several thousand earnest men to the Association.

One grand element of strength is shown by this organization—namely: The absolute equality of its members. They have not permitted designing men to foster and establish a set of so-called "High-Class Runs" among them to breed discord and disunion. One switchman is the same as another, and a thousand are but as one, in all the essential points that originally brought them together. Other railway labor organizations have allowed grades and castes to grow up in their Orders, those of the lower grade having scarcely any rights that the others are bound to respect and assist them to maintain. Not so with the switchmen; the young blood in their Association will enable them to steer clear of the rocks and shoals that are sadly trying the timbers of the older Orders.

In the strike upon the Burlington system this Association was not officially connected, and had no part whatever in the management or final settlement of that trouble.

> "We know what Master laid thy keel,
> What workman wrought thy ribs of steel,
> Who made each mast and sail and rope,
> What anvils rang, what hammers beat,
> In what a forge, and what a heat,
> Were shaped the anchors of thy hope."

THE GREAT STRIKE.

In order to give our readers an intelligent understanding of the causes that led to the strike, it will be necessary to state that for a number of years an iniquitous system of classification had been in vogue on the Chicago Burlington & Quincy lines—a system under which gross injustice was done to engineers and firemen, in that they were so graded that their wages were reduced far below the average of the recognized standard of pay on ninety per cent of the roads in the United States and Canada.

For years the men were dissatisfied; all along the lines could be heard the mutterings of discontent. The complaints touching the grievances were universal; and these complaints expanded into proportions of the gravest character. The tendency of the agitation was toward organized action. Engineers and firemen realized the necessity of co-operation, and, as a consequence, committees of the two Brotherhoods were convened in Chicago, in the month of January, 1888. Joint action was decided upon as the basis of operation. S. E. Hoge was selected as Chairman of the Engineers' Committee, and J. H. Murphy as Chairman of the Firemen.

The following schedule of grievances was prepared, which met with the unanimous approval of the joint committees. This schedule was presented to the officials of the Chicago, Burlington & Quincy road in a spirit of moderation and fairness. Every proposition had been carefully considered, and there was no disposition to take any undue advantage of the company.

BROTHERHOOD'S SCHEDULE.

Revised Schedule of Wages Governing the Pay of Engineers and Firemen on the Chicago, Burlington & Quincy Railroad and Operated Lines, Presented to the General Managers on February 15, 1888, by Committee of Engineers and Firemen.

Article I.

No engineer or fireman shall be suspended or discharged without just or sufficient cause; and in case an engineer or fireman believes his discharge or suspension to have been unjust, he shall make out a written statement of the facts in the premises, and submit it to his Master Mechanic, and at the same time designate any other engineer or fireman (as the accused may wish) who may be in the employ of the Company ; and the Master Mechanic, together with the engineer or fireman last referred to, shall, in conjunction with the Superintendent, investigate the case in question without unnecessary delay, and render a prompt decision ; and in case the aforesaid discharge or suspension is decided to be unjust, he (the accused) shall be at once reinstated, and shall be paid for all time lost on such account.

Article II.

SECTION 1. Engineers and firemen shall be called at a reasonable time before leaving time. The caller shall have a book, in which the engineer and fireman must register their names and time when called. Engineers' and firemen's time shall commence when they take charge of the engine ; or, if the engine is not ready, the time they report at the office for duty, and shall end at the time designated on roundhouse

register as arriving, or otherwise relieved from duty. Time
shall be taken from roundhouse register, instead of conduct-
or's register or train-sheet.

SEC. 2. When engineers or firemen are ordered out,
and not used on account of train being abandoned, or other
causes, the engineer or fireman called on duty shall receive
pay for one-half ($\frac{1}{2}$) day for five (5) hours or less, and stand
first out.

Article III.

SECTION 1. All passenger engineers running four-wheel
connected engines shall receive three and one-half ($3\frac{1}{2}$) cents
per mile; six-wheel connected engines, three and eight-
tenths (3 8-10) cents per mile.

All passenger firemen firing four-wheel connected en-
gineslshall receive two and one-tenth (2 1-10) cents per mile;
six-wheel connected engines, two and one-fourth ($2\frac{1}{4}$) cents
per mile.

One hundred miles or less to be considered a day's
work; over one hundred miles, at the same rate per mile.

SEC. 2. All freight engineers running four-wheel connected engines, four (4) cents per mile; six-wheel connected
engines, four and three-tenths (4 3-10) cents per mile.

All freight firemen, firing four-wheel connected engines,
two and four-tenths (2 4-10) cents per mile; six-wheel connected engines, two-and six tenths (2 6-10) cents per mile.
One hundred miles or less to constitute a day's work. Over
one hundred miles at the same rate per mile.

SEC. 3. Engineers running consolidated (eight-wheel
connected) engines, four and one-half ($4\frac{1}{2}$) cents per mile.

Firemen firing consolidated engines, two and four-
tenths (2 4-10) cents per mile, two firemen on each consolidated engine. One hundred miles or less to constitute a day's
work. Over one hundred miles at the same rate per mile.

SEC. 4. On freight runs which occupy more than ten
(10) hours to the one hundred miles, overtime shall be paid
at the rate of forty (40) cents per hour for engineers, and
twenty-four (24) cents per hour for firemen.

SEC. 5. Local freight runs on Middle Iowa Division
will be allowed one trip and one-half ($1\frac{1}{2}$) each way; overtime
to be allowed after being on the road fifteen (15) hours.

Article IV.

SECTION 1. In computing the delayed time, the first hour shall not be counted, but if delayed one hour and thirty minutes, shall be counted as two hours, and any fraction of thirty minutes, or over, thereafter, shall be considered one hour.

Engineers on freight to be paid forty (40) cents per hour; firemen on freight, twenty-four (24) cents per hour. Engineers on passenger, thirty-five (35) cents per hour; firemen on passenger, twenty-one (21) cents per hour.

This article refers only to delays before starting and after arriving at terminals.

SEC. 2. Engineers and Firemen called to go to Transfers or Junction Points before card time, delayed time shall commence from time of leaving roundhouse.

Article V.

On passenger runs that do not exceed three dollars and seventy-five cents ($3.75) per day, engineers shall receive three dollars and seventy-five cents ($3.75), and firemen two dollars and twenty-five cents ($2.25) per day; overtime shall be allowed in same proportion when on duty over twelve (12) hours in making such runs. In case actual mileage exceed $3.75, actual mileage at the rate of three and one-half ($3\frac{1}{2}$) cents for engineers, and two and one-tenth (2 1-10) cents for firemen per mile shall be allowed.

Article VI.

Short freight runs of less then eighty (80) miles when doubled within twelve hours, mileage allowed according to Sec. 2, Article III, and if not doubled within twelve hours to be allowed one day each way.

Article VII.

All engineers and firemen of work trains or helpers to be paid three dollars and fifty cents ($3.50) per day for engineers, and two dollars and ten cents (2.10) per day for firemen; twelve hours or less, one hundred miles or less, to be called a day's work. If the run should exceed one hundred miles, full freight rates as per class of engine for the entire run.

Article VIII.

SECTION 1. Engineers in snow-plow service (when on duty) shall be paid at the rate of six ($6.00) dollars per day, and

3

firemen in snow-plow service shall be paid at the rate of three dollars and sixty cents ($3.60) per day; ten hours or less to constitute a day's work; all over ten hours to be paid at the rate of sixty (60) cents per hour for engineers, and thirty-six (36) cents per hour for firemen. When engines in snow-plow service are held in roundhouse subject to call for service, the engineer of said engine shall be paid four dollars ($4.00), and firemen two dollars and forty cents ($2.40) per day, of twenty-four (24) hours or less.

SEC. 2.   Engineers and firemen on weed-destroying engines shall be paid at the same rates as in snow-plow service.

SEC. 3.   Engineers and firemen on surburban trains between Chicago and Downers Grove will receive, the engineer one dollar and seventy-five cents ($1.75), and the firemen one dollar and five cents ($1.05) for each round trip.

Article IX.

Switch engineers to receive three dollars and firemen one dollar and eighty cents per day, of twelve hours or less; all over twelve hours to be paid, the engineer thirty cents per hour and the fireman eighteen cents per hour; except in Chicago and Kansas City yards, where ten (10) hours or less will constitute a day's work, at $3.00 for engineer and $1.80 for fireman per day; thirty cents (30) for engineers and eighteen cents (18) for firemen per hour for all over ten (10) hours. Any fraction of thirty minutes, or over, shall be counted one hour.

They shall have regular engines, and shall not be taken off to give work to extra men.

Article X.

Where engineers and firemen are compelled to double hills, they shall receive one hour's pay per double, at the rate of forty cents for engineers and twenty-four cents for firemen.

Article XI.

Hostlers shall be paid at the rate of two dollars and forty cents per day; twelve hours or less to constitute a day's work. All over twelve hours to be paid at the rate of twenty-four cents per hour.

They shall not be required to knock fires.

Hostlers to be provided at all terminal points.

In all cases where engineers and firemen have to watch their engines, they shall be paid at the full rate per hour.

Article XII.

SECTION 1. Engineers and firemen taking light engines over the road, or dead-heading over the road on company business, will be paid passenger rates; and where light engines are taken over the road, a flagman is to be furnished.

In case engineers or firemen are to attend court, or on any company business, engineers to receive four dollars per day and expenses, and firemen two dollars and forty cents per day and expenses.

SEC. 2. That no engineer or fireman be required to pull any train without a conductor, or a man to take charge of said train.

Article XIII.

Engineers and firemen will run, first in, first out, and, as far as practicable, on their respective divisions; and where engines are pooled, not to be governed by train department.

Article XIV.

Rights to regular runs, when ability is equal, will be governed by seniority. Engineers and firemen having regular runs up to the Agreement of 1886 will not be affected by this Article.

Article XV.

No more extra engineers or firemen will be assigned than is necessary to move the traffic with promptness and dispatch, and should any engineer or fireman feel himself aggrieved by the assignment of too many men, he can proceed as in Article I, but will receive no pay for loss of time.

Galesburg Division engineers and firemen will not be required to run east of Aurora.

Article XVI.

No road engineer or fireman will be expected to do regular yard work at terminal stations. In the event of their being called upon to do said work, the engineer shall receive forty (40) cents per hour, and the fireman twenty-four (24) cents per hour.

Article XVII.

No fines shall be assessed against engineers or firemen.

Article XVIII.

That engineers and firemen and their families be given transportation when applied for, and that some arrangement be made to pass Brotherhood men over the road.

Article XIX.

SECTION 1. That where time is not allowed, the Master Mechanic shall cause the trip report to be returned to the engineer or fireman sending it in, stating why the time is not allowed, as soon as practicable.

SEC. 2. All officers, engineers and firemen will observe strict courtesy of manners in their intercourse with each other.

Article XX.

All road engines will be provided with cracked coal suitable for firing, and the company shall do all outside cleaning, and where engines are pooled, the company to do all the cleaning.

Article XXI.

Engineers and firemen shall not be required to go out when they need rest, and they are expected to judge for themselves whether they need rest or not.

Article XXII.

It is understood that there will be no more examinations or tests, except such as are agreed upon by the General Manager and the General Grievance Committee.

Article XXIII.

That on the adoption of this schedule, it shall be kept posted in a conspicuous place in all register rooms on the line of road.

All previous schedules and contracts shall be considered void.

(Signed)   S. E. HOGE, *Chairman Engineers.*
                 J. H. MURPHY, *Chairman Firemen.*

It will readily be seen that the engineers and firemen request that the compensation be fixed by the

mile, as that is the method adopted by nine-tenths of
the railroads in the United States.

The Burlington officials have said that this compensation was sought by the Brotherhoods without regard to other conditions or circumstances. This
position of the company will not bear inspection.
For instance: in cases of high-class runs which they
have cited, taking only a few hours for the trip, engineers and firemen have been compelled to care for
their own engines; in fact, keep up the repairs of
the engine, thereby saving to the company the cost of
a hostler, and keeping the engine in constant use
without the aid of the machinist. It was not sought
by the Brotherhoods to create these high-class runs;
on the contrary, the desire was to do away with
them. Article XI. of the foregoing schedule plainly
says that hostlers must be provided at terminal
points, and where absolutely necessary for the engineer and fireman to perform this duty, that they be
paid the full rate per hour. It was evidently the desire of the men to force these so-called high-class
runs off the schedule, while the company desired to
retain them. It is also seen that while the Brotherhoods asked for compensation according to the miles
run, the trip pay could still have been continued,
providing that the company did not require them to
do the work of roundhouse men and machinists. The
only question involved here is, that this company
should pay as much per trip of equal length as is
paid by the other important lines of the country. If
the desire had been to pay the men honestly and

fairly, it was immaterial whether the compensation be by the trip or mile. To illustrate: If a passenger engineer runs one hundred miles, this schedule calls for three dollars and fifty cents. This rate is paid by the C., R. I. & P., A., T. & S. F., Wabash, and in fact ninety per cent. of the great railway systems in the United States. The Burlington, not desiring to pay upon a basis that would make a fair comparison of wages with those of other companies, abandons the mile schedule, and simply says: "We will pay you three dollars for the trip;" in other words, three cents per mile for the same service for which other roads pay three and one-half cents.

It is true that the Brotherhoods have demanded in this schedule "a considerable average increase of pay," but the public must understand that they did not demand this increase from the Burlington over what is paid by its competitors in business. Had the Burlington conceded this increase of pay, it would only have been called upon to pay precisely what its neighbors and rivals have been paying for years. A large average increase of pay must be made before the employes of this road are placed upon an equal footing with those of other roads. For many years the Burlington road had the advantage of a first-class equipment of enginemen at rates of pay far below what its competitors have been compelled to pay for the same service.

In strict justice, these men might have demanded restitution, but they only asked for honest treatment in the future. They did not ask for the abolishment of classification based upon merit, age or experience.

The proposition is substantially this: If an engineer is compelled to pull the best train on the Burlington road, he should have the best pay. It is not material whether he has been an engineer one year or ten years—competency alone is the requisite.

When the company places a man in charge of one of its great express trains, and intrusts to his skill and judgment the lives and property of its patrons, by that very act it certifies that he is a first-class engineer, and entitled to receive pay accordingly. A first-year man is not necessarily a man of inferior ability; the company would not risk its own property and reputation, nor would the public risk their lives, with third-rate men. Why, then, should the company insist on paying them third-class wages? It is injustice, imposition, and avarice! The man who is able to perform the work of a first-class engineer should receive first-class pay, whatever that may be; and he is a slave who accepts less.

On the other hand the company takes this position: It places a man in a position which requires at his hands the skill, knowledge and ability of a first-class engineer. The first year it pays him much less than a first-class engineer's wages; the second year it slightly advances his wages, but still keeps them below that of the first-class; the third year he is paid their highest wages to an engineer (which is still less than that paid by other roads), having done the same character and quality of work for three years. The result is that the company is continually gaining from the men who are in their first and sec-

ond year's service a large per cent of wages. It thus
gains all the percentages in this scheme, because a
number of men who work the first or second year do
not remain long enough in the employ of this company to be entitled to the wages that are paid to the
men who have served their third year. These first
and second year men who resign to accept better positions on other roads, enter other occupations in life,
or are crippled, killed, or discharged by the company,
are replaced by other first and second year men, and
the company is thus enabled to keep a large percent-
age of employes at greatly reduced rates of wages.
No objection could be offered to paying those who
had been employed on the road a long time an extra
gratuity if so desired, nor could complaint be made
if, in its generosity, the company wished to pension
men who had served it faithfully a number of years;
but when this gratuity (?), this generosity (?), is only a
small portion of the sum stolen from the same employes, the men were only human and failed to
appreciate the kindness intended.

One of two things must be true: either that the
engineers were first-class men entitled to first-class
pay, or that the public was deceived when it was
asked to travel upon or risk property on trains run
by second and third grade, and, consequently inferior
men. The latter could not be maintained by the
company. Every General Manager in the Western
country knows that the Chicago, Burlington & Quincy
road was equipped with first-class men in these de-
partments, second to none anywhere. This is clearly

proven by their general eagerness to re-engage the former employes of this company. Mr. Jeffrey, General Manager of the Illinois Central road, and Chairman of the General Managers' Association, stated that in the future all vacancies upon his line would be held for the ex-employes of the Burlington road. Nor is Mr. Jeffrey an exception in this matter; the C., R. I. & P., C., S. F. & C., C. & N.-W., C. M. & St. P., Wisconsin Central, M. & N. W., C., A. & St. L., together with the Eastern lines, are rapidly receiving these men into their employ.

What has been said in relation to the engineers applies also to the firemen, because upon all the roads the fireman's wages is based upon those of the engineer, and he receives from fifty-five to sixty per cent of the wages that is paid to the engineer; therefore, a shaving down of the engineer's pay means also a shaving down of the amount paid to the fireman, so that on all sides the peculiar system adopted by the Burlington road robs both classes and enriches its own treasury.

In the circular issued by the company it says: "The company reserves the right to ascertain by whatever examinations it may think advisable, whether its employes of all classes are capable of fulfilling the duties they undertake, and the public also demand that the railroad company shall take every precaution to employ only those men who can safely perform the work entrusted to them." This was one of the main points at issue. When the company had made such examinations, and found that an engineer

or fireman was capable of taking charge of an engine,
and that he was competent to fill the company's obligation to the public, what right, in justice, had they
to ask that the man accept a lower grade of compensation? He performed the same service rendered
by the older men, or those who had been longer on the
road, and, in justice, should have received the same
pay. If sent out on freight runs, he performed harder
service, and a service that required skill and judgment equal at least to the passenger engineer, and
should have been paid accordingly in strict sense of
justice and equity.

The question now arises, had these men just
cause to complain? Were the engineers and firemen
of the Burlington road seeking to take any undue
advantage of that corporation? Were they as well
paid as the employes of other roads performing similar
services?

We invite the attention of the public to the following comparisons:

On the "Q" road there is a round trip between
Rockford and Aurora which is made twenty-six times
a month by the engineer.

On the North-Western road there is a round trip
between Rockford and Chicago which is also made
twenty-six times per month.

The North-Western round trip is twenty-two miles
greater than the "Q" round trip. The North-Western
engineer travels 572 miles per month more than the
"Q's" engineer.

At the rate of compensation asked by the engineers

—viz : 3½ cts. per mile—the North-Western road should only pay $20.02 per month to the engineer on the Rockford-to-Chicago trip greater than that paid to the "Q" engineer who runs on the Rockford-to-Aurora trip. But the fact is that the "Q" road pays its engineer $104 per month, while the North-Western pays its engineer $175. The "Q" engineer holds just as responsible a position as the engineer on the North-Western. He has to cross three intersecting roads in the making of his trip, and, in addition to his work as an engineer, the labor of hostling or caring for the engine is imposed upon him, while the engineer for the North-Western is not obliged to care for his engine. The latter's work begins when he jumps on the engine at one end of the trip, and ceases when he delivers it at the other end.

The engineer on the Sterling Branch run draws $84.10 for ninety-eight miles. He stops in Rock Falls six hours, and takes care of his own engine. The engineer that runs the Batavia and Geneva accommodation receives $87.10, and the Chicago & North-Western pays for like runs $96.20, the distance being two miles greater on the Chicago, Burlington & Quincy.

The reason we ask more pay for the branch runs is to compensate the men for the extra work done on account of the engineers having to do the work of a machinist.

The engineer on the Rockford way-freight runs nightly (twenty-six nights constituting one month), for which he receives $56.00 ; fireman, $35.00 per month.

The engineers on the fast mail, Chicago, Burlington & Quincy, 125 miles per day, receive $97.50 for twenty-six days' time. The engineers on the Chicago & North-Western, for the same service, receive $120.00.

The runs on the main line of the Chicago, Burlington & Quincy, 125 miles per day, thirty-five days per month, amount received, $131.00. On the trunk lines out of Chicago, for the same service, the engineers receive $161.00.

The engineers on the Buda and Vermont Branch of the "Q" line, 188 3-10 miles per day, twenty-six days constituting one month, receive for same $125.50. The Chicago & North-Western Railway pays for like service $181.00.

We desire further to state that no first-class engineer on the Chicago & North-Western receives less than $96.20 for twenty-six days' work, if ready for duty.

The Rock Island road pays its engineers on all of its passenger trains $3.60, and its firemen $2.15 for the 100-mile run.

The Quincy road only pays $3.50 for this same run to the engineers on a few of its heaviest trains—like the Kansas City one—and on all other trains it pays only $3.37½. It only pays its firemen $2.00 when with the engineer who is paid $3.50, and $1.90 when with the engineer who receives $3.37½.

The Rock Island road pays $4.15 for a run of one hundred miles to its freight engineers, and does not require them to act as hostlers for their engines.

The Quincy road pays its freight engineer on the 101-mile run from Galva to New Boston $3.75. This

run is on a branch road, and the engineer is compelled
to do hostler's duty for his engine at both ends of
his run.

Let us compare two short runs: The first is on
the Chicago, Milwaukee & St. Paul road. The round
trip between Chicago and Elgin is seventy-four miles,
for which the engineer is paid $3.70. The engineer
has full control of his time every second day, and has
not to act as hostler for his engine. The second is
on the "Q" road. The round trip between Chicago
and Aurora is seventy-seven miles. The engineer is
paid $3.35. He has to "hostle" his engine, and his
entire time belongs to the road. Some days he has
to be under the orders for eighteen hours per day.

Complaint is made in the road's circular because
we asked that "Galesburg Division engineers and
firemen be not required to run east of Aurora." The
idea sought to be conveyed by the company is that
this request is unreasonable, and calculated to impose greater expense on the road. The fact is that
compliance with this request will not impose one cent
of extra expense on the road. No objection has been
offered to running the engines through from Galesburg to Chicago. The change of crews—engineers
and firemen—at Aurora will not increase the company's outlay. There are about 300 of the engineers
and firemen who live in Aurora. Many of these men
own homes; some of these homes, however, are not
entirely paid for. If they are compelled to run from
Galesburg to Chicago and return, they would have to
sacrifice their property, and remove either to Gales-

burg or to Chicago. They ask that the crews be made
to run on the one end of the route only from Chicago
to Aurora and return, and on the other end only from
Galesburg to Aurora and return. If we were paid on
the mile system, the change of crews would not cost
the road one cent.

It is also complained that we ask that some
arrangements be made in relation to passing Brotherhood men on the "Q" trains. We make no demand
in this regard. Our purpose in making this request
was to get some uniform rule put in force on this road,
the same as prevails on other roads. We have no
right to demand this. We did not demand it; our
desire was, while we were negotiating, to get this
question, now unsettled, so determined that the conductors would hereafter know precisely what to do,
and thus be able to avoid conflicts.

On the Pan Handle road the freight engineer who
runs from Indianapolis to Bradford, a distance of 105
miles, receives $4.25 for the trip; his fireman receives
$2.15.

On the "Q" road the round trip run from Galesburg to Peoria is 105 miles, for which the engineer receives $3.60 and the fireman $2.10.

From Quincy to Colchester the round trip is 107
miles. The "Q" road pays its engineer for that trip
$3.75, and its fireman $2.15.

For runs of 100 miles on the Union Pacific road
the engineer on passenger trains receives $3.85. The
"Q" road is a competitor of the Union Pacific, and
for a long distance travels over parallel lines through

country of precisely the same character.   Yet we have
only asked $3.50 per 100 miles for a passenger engi-
neer on the "Q" road.

SUBMITTING THE PROPOSITIONS.

The requests of the men were met with indifference
at the hands of the Burlington officials.   Not the slightest encouragement was given to the Committees.
They were given to understand, substantially, that no
concessions on the part of the company need be
expected.   The abominable system of classification,
the chief source of complaint, would be continued,
and the protests of the men, however emphatic or
unanimous, would not prevail.

FURTHER EFFORTS TO SECURE JUSTICE.

The Committees having exhausted every expedient
to effect an amicable adjustment, appealed to their
Grand Executive Officers to come to the rescue.
Grand Chief Arthur and Grand Master Sargent
responded to the call.   The Joint Committee was
convened by the Grand Officers, and a careful analy-
sis of the grievances was made.   Having satisfied
themselves that the demands of the men were reasonable and just, the Grand Officers, accompanied by
the Joint Committee, called upon the officials of the C.,
B. & Q. system.   A protracted interview followed,
which resulted practically in a failure, as the officials
declined to accede to a single proposition of the Committee, notwithstanding numerous modifications were
made in the interest of harmony.   The interview
ended abruptly upon the declaration of General Man-

ager Stone, that he would not accede to any part of the
proposition bearing upon classification. In this, he
was emphatic and uncompromising. This ended the
conference so far as General Manager Stone was concerned, and the Committee respectfully withdrew.

STILL FURTHER EFFORTS IN THE INTEREST OF HARMONY AND JUSTICE.

Grand Chief Arthur and Grand Master Sargent,
realizing that the difficulty had assumed a most serious phase, decided, upon consultation, to make a final
effort to avert what now seemed inevitable—a strike.
A telegraphic dispatch was transmitted to President
Perkins, at Boston, appealing to him to do justice by
his men and avert the impending strike. His answer
was evasive, indefinite, showing an utter indifference
as to what the result might be.

NEARING THE CRISIS.

Having now been cut off from every avenue lead-
ing to an honorable adjustment of grievances, having
exhausted every reasonable expedient to prevent
trouble, the Committee, with the sanction of the
Grand Officers, decided that the engineers and firemen
should withdraw in a body from the service of the
company, at 4 o'clock, on Monday morning, February 27, unless some disposition was shown to
remedy the grievances of the men. On Sunday,
February 26, the day previous to the inauguration
of the strike, Chairmen Hoge and Murphy called upon
General Manager Stone, and informed him of the
action of the Committee, again appealing to him to

render justice to the men. The General Manager arbitrarily declined to make any concessions, or to give the Committee any satisfaction, and here the matter ended with the final conference, with the strike inevitable and its consequences in full view.

THE STRIKE.

On Monday morning, the 27th instant, at 4 o'clock, the strike began, all engineers and firemen on the entire system withdrawing from the service of the company. All trains on the road at that hour were taken to their terminal points. The men had exhibited throughout, patience, prudence and forbearance, and the strike at once became monumental of an infamous policy on the part of a rich and powerful corporation to rob its trusted employes of money earned, that it might increase its profits, and with equal distinctness does the strike record the fact that a great body of workingmen sought by every honorable means to secure their rights, preferring to suffer than to be longer degraded.

THE PRESS.

No sooner was the strike inaugurated than the press began to manipulate public opinion. The most sensational reports were concocted and published throughout the length and breadth of the land; and while at the inception of the strike there seemed to be a disposition to treat the men fairly, it was not long before a change of sentiment pervaded the utterances of the press, and fair-dealing and honest criticism gave place to the grossest misrepresentations, with the evident purpose of arousing public opinion against the strikers, thereby making them the victims of the corporation they were struggling against, and of which it was the subsidized agent and representative.

When the switchmen joined the engineers and firemen, March 23, for a short time there was a change in the tone of the press reports. They evidently feared a repetition of the lawlessness of the strikes of 1877, but when they found that the switchmen, too, were a law-abiding class of men, they again acknowledged allegiance to the corporation. Reporters were sent to the meetings of the strikers, who, believing that they would be fairly dealt with, had appointed a Press Committee. In almost every instance the papers failed to print the matter as given to the reporters, and in many cases did print exactly the reverse. This Press Committee, composed of conservative men, soon learned that the reporters went directly from them to the Burlington officials, where the interviews were inspected and put in proper shape to answer the purposes of the company. An effort was then made by the Press Committee to get their communications directly to the papers, without the use of the reporters. In a short time this also failed. Chiefs Arthur and Sargent and Chairmen Hoge and Murphy, at the Grand Pacific Hotel, had a similar experience. It was impossible to get proper representation of the facts printed. March 26 one paper accepted and printed a communication from the Press Committee, but from that time on nothing was printed verbatim. The article referred to is herewith given:

"As the Burlington Bureau of Information has ceased to give out facts, but are drawing on advertising material, we wish to state the causes of their trouble with the switchmen. They have not struck, but have left the service of that company. 'Self-preservation is the first law of nature.' This is the reason in a nutshell. For the past week every switch engine in the house has been out. Three have gone in again disabled, and less than half of the regular work has been done. As long as the company were satisfied to let the men take time to insure safety there was no trouble. But as the cars accumulated in the yards, they considered it necessary to push the men beyond the point of safety, against their protests, and the 'strike' or stoppage was the result. A few of the engineers and firemen are locomotive men, but the majority are not, and all are ignorant of our signals and methods of work. In switching cars there should be no one in the cab but the engineer and fireman, and both should be watching the movements and signals of the switchmen. As it is now, the fireman stands in the gangway, while his seat is occupied by two or three Pinkerton men. No signal can be seen from that side of the engine. The engineer keeps his window closed, to shut out the taunts of passers-by, and the switchmen are left to take their chances. As long as he was allowed to pull pins with the train at a stand-still, and make couplings with the engine attached, he could do the work with reasonable safety, but this is not the manner of handling cars on our western roads, and would not have been tolerated one month ago.   Aside from pulling pins and coupling cars, there is the continual danger of collisions, as at Hawthorne, last Thursday night, when switch engine 176 was run through by a road engine and train, whose engineer did not see stop-signals nor the headlight ahead of him on a straight track. The tracks in and about Chicago are cut up with railroad crossings, semaphores, connections and the interlocking switch systems.   These new engineers know nothing about them, and are continually running through and under them, to the imminent danger of themselves, switchmen and opposing trains. These varied sources of danger to life and limb are so great that the men are undoubtedly justified in leaving the service of that company."

THE FIRST BOYCOTT.

From a circular issued in June, by the Brotherhood of Engineers the following is taken:

"Shortly after the inauguration of the strike, reports were received at headquarters to the effect that certain lines of railway, parallel to the C., B. & Q., were hauling the cars and handling the traffic of that company.   These reports created decidedly bitter feeling on the part of the striking employes, and ultimated in the convening of the chairmen of the Grievance Committees of the several systems complained of.   At this meeting, which took place at Chicago, on March 5, it was agreed that the engineers and firemen employed on said systems should serve notice on their respective officials, through the proper committees, that while they were willing to perform all their legitimate duties, they would decline thenceforth to haul C., B. & Q. cars, or transact any of the business properly devolving upon that company, as by so doing, they would virtually be taking the positions vacated by their striking brethren, and by that means contribute to their defeat, while at the same time they would be giving aid and comfort to the corporation against which they were struggling for their rights.

THE QUESTION OF LAW INTRODUCED.

"Out of this action of the Committees arose a series of the most threatening complications, which it may be well to explain at this point. It should be understood, in the first place, that there is upon the statute books of Illinois a law which provides that any officer, chairman or leader of a labor organization, association or combination, who advises or causes a body of employes to withdraw their services from any company or corporation, thereby crippling the business or interfering with the operations of the said company or corporation, shall be deemed guilty of conspiracy, and shall be fined or imprisoned in proportion to the extent of the injury caused. It will be observed that the provisions of this law were exceedingly embarrassing to the Grand Officers; and upon taking legal advice they found, to their discomfiture, that they were even then occupying untenable ground and exposing themselves to the liability of being prosecuted under the conspiracy act referred.to. Not only this, but it soon became apparent that the action taken by the Committee on March 5 did not meet with the unanimous approval of the engineers and firemen employed on the several systems there represented. On the contrary, the engineers and firemen on some of the lines positively refused to be bound by the agreement, and openly avowed their intention to perform any and all duties that might be required of them, including the handling of C., B. & Q. business.

WANT OF UNITY AND HARMONY.

"The lack of unanimity at this particular juncture proved fatal to any good results that might have followed concert of action in carrying out the instructions of the Committee. Division, discontent and disorder soon began to appear. There was a total lack of harmony in the spirit and purpose of the men, and those who were disposed to act in good faith and refuse to handle C., B. & C. traffic simply laid themselves liable to dismissal from the service of the company, without assurance or hope of protection or support from the men employed on the same system.

STRIKE ON THE SANTA FE.

"Under this condition of affairs occurred the noted strike on the Sante Fe system, which was precipitated on March 16, on account of the alleged aid given the C., B. & Q. by that company in hauling its cars and transacting its business. Upon a more careful investigation of the matter, it was found that there was no adequate cause for the strike—that it grew out of a

misapprehension of the facts in the case, and on March
18, after being out two days, the men returned to work
in a body, the road resumed operations, and the same
satisfactory relations between the company and the
men which had hitherto prevailed, were restored.

THE SWITCHMEN.

"From the very inception of the strike, the members of the Switchmen's Mutual Aid Association
evinced a profound interest in the struggle and freely
tendered their sympathy and support to the strikers.
They realized that the contest was for the maintenance of a common cause, and that the employes in
every department of the railway service were interested in the result. The Grand Master, J. L. Monaghan, prompted by a desire to protect the interests of
his men, as well as to extend a helping hand to his
co-laborers, came to the front nobly, and with the aid
of the members of his Order, took a decided stand in
favor of the strikers. The switchmen realized that
their interests were largely at stake, that a victory for
the strikers meant a victory for them, and *vice versa*,
and, with this feeling, they left the service of the
company in a body, preferring to sacrifice their situations rather than serve in the employ of a company
that refused to do common justice to its employes.
Candor compels the admission, that we are indebted
to the switchmen for aid freely given in the hour of
our direst necessity. They acted the part of manly
men, and are entitled to the thanks and gratitude of
the Brotherhoods."

Equal candor on the part of those who signed the above circular would compel the admission that the switchmen have not yet received that which was so freely promised them during the early days of March and on the night of March 22,—namely, federation.

From the 1st of March until the 22d, Mr. Monaghan was in frequent consultation with Chiefs Arthur and Sargent. It was evident that the switchmen in remaining at work with the new engineers were doing the cause an incalculable injury, and efforts were made to overcome this new difficulty.

FEDERATION.

The switchmen and the brakemen were willing and anxious to unite with the Brotherhood. They did not wish the company to be victorious through aid given by them, and they were equally unwilling to give aid to the Brotherhood in this struggle and receive what many had received in the past, only injury. In this condition of affairs an arrangement was made whereby, in future troubles, the two Brotherhoods and the Association of Switchmen were to stand faithfully by each other. It was at this time the universal opinion among the switchmen, engineers and firemen that some such plan should be devised, and the Constitutions changed accordingly, and this feeling was concurred in by the officers of the three organizations. The legal counsel was called into the conference and a plan formulated for future action, which was to be subject to the

Annual Convention of each organization. True to the promises given by Grand Master Sargent, the Convention of Firemen did, in September, 1888, put forward a most comprehensive plan of fedration, which was adopted by the Convention of Switchmen in the same month, and which apparently died at the Convention of Engineers in October.

Whatever the action since taken, the switchmen were then perfectly satisfied—particularly so, as at the union meeting held in Chicago on the night of March 22, prominent members of the two Brotherhoods from all parts of the United States gave their unqualified approval to the action of their officers, and, furthermore, pledged the honor of the Brotherhoods that the obligation would be faithfully met and promptly carried out. More solemn or binding obligations were never entered into by men. The switchmen were promised, and written pledges given by the officers of the Brotherhoods, that the same financial assistance given to the engineers engaged in the strike should also be given to them, as long as an engineer received a dollar, the switchmen should receive a like amount.

SWITCHMEN ENTER THE STRIKE.

On the morning of March 23 the switchmen, with the consent of Grand Master Monaghan, left the service of the Burlington Company in Chicago, not one single man remaining behind. Out of seventeen yardmasters, eleven went with the switchmen. Two of these, however, remained out but a few days, and then returned to the service of the company. Of the switchmen, but one returned.

ALONG THE LINE.

Messengers were immediately dispatched over the system to notify the switchmen what action had at last been decided upon, and these, with few exceptions, took the same course as was taken by their Chicago brethren. At Aurora, Galesburg, Burlington, Ottumwa, Creston, Plattsmouth, Omaha, Lincoln, Kansas City, St. Joe, Beardstown, and all points where switch engines are employed, the men, with few exceptions, made the sacrifice required of them, and did it freely. At Quincy the men also went out; but on an offer of the agent to increase their pay, all but five returned to work. It is gratifying to the rest of the men to know that this promise was never fulfilled to the Quincy switchmen.

BRAKEMEN.

The brakemen did not go out in this movement, as was expected by the switchmen. Written pledges were offered them by the Brotherhoods, similar to those accepted by the Switchmen. Mr. Wilkinson did not feel like assuming the responsibility of calling his men out on the strength of these pledges.

The constitution gave him no such authority and he did not feel like taking the responsibility of doing an unconstitutional act.

The feeling among those actually engaged in the strike is friendly toward the Brotherhood of Brakemen. They know that these men were not opposed to them, although they remained in the service of the Company.

SECOND BOYCOTT.

Immediately after the switchmen left the service of the C., B. & Q. corporation, a meeting of yard engineers, firemen and switchmen was held at Chicago,

at which it was agreed that no C., B. & Q. cars should
be handled from and after that time. Upon the taking
effect of this agreement, it became apparent that the
yardmen would not receive the support of many of the
road men in carrying out its provisions; in fact, it
was currently reported, and not denied, that upon
certain lines the road men had decided to handle the
business of the C., B. & Q., in the event of the yard
men declining to do so. This division in the policy
of the men created the most intense dissatisfaction,
and gave rise to deep indignation. The men who
declined to handle C., B. & Q. cars were given to understand that dismissal would be the penalty if they
persisted in carrying out that policy. Other men
were ready to perform their duties. To adhere to the
agreement meant the sacrifice of their situations. A
number of them had already been dismissed. De-
moralization and dismay, the fruit of discord and disunion, were beginning to take root.

ON THE C., M. & ST. P. RAILWAY

this agreement was more faithfully carried out.
When the yard engineers refused to handle "Q" cars
they were at once joined by the switchmen and yardmasters (including the General Yardmaster). Switch-
tenders, road engineers and firemen, brakemen, and
most of the conductors were entirely in accord with
them. The result was a general closing down of
business on the road. The men were discharged, and
fully one-third of the entire force of the road laid off.

The company evidently intended to clear the decks for a great battle.

It has been repeatedly claimed, that if the other roads centering in Chicago had made the prompt action of the C., M. & St. P. men general, the boycott, with all that the term implies would have been on to the fullest extent.

A NEW DEPARTURE

was demanded to avert the gravest complications, which seemed inevitable. A meeting was called, and counsel was taken from those who were in position to map out a new and better line of action. This meeting was addressed by the Grand Master of the Switchmen's Association, the Grand Master of the Brotherhood of Locomotive Firemen, General Manager Jeffery of the Illinois Central, and others. The situation was clearly defined, the peril of continuing in a hopeless crusade against C., B. & Q. cars was vividly outlined, and, as a result of the meeting, traffic was resumed upon the several railways the following morning, and all those who had been dismissed for refusing to handle C., B. & Q. cars were reinstated in their former positions. Much unjust criticism has been passed upon this action, and yet we feel confident that if the situation and surrounding conditions had been half understood, it would have met with universal approval.

It must be remembered that unity of action had not been secured, and there was no authority in the Brotherhood to enforce it, even if the chief so-willed, which he evidently did not. Under the circumstances, to continue the boycott against "Q" cars was to destroy or divide the Brotherhood; the men were not yet educated up to the point of making so great a sacrifice, or at least what they considered a sacrifice.

And yet, if this unity of action had been attained, if not one Brotherhood man in the United States had taken another's place who refused to handle "Q" cars, where was the power to defeat them? Such a power does not exist! Not even in the General Government.

KNIGHTS OF LABOR.

At the very outset of the strike it was claimed by the Burlington management that Knights of Labor stood ready to supplant the Brotherhoods upon their lines. This has been proven to be a misrepresentation to a very great extent. It was true, however, that there was considerable feeling existing between the Knights of Labor and the Brotherhood of Engineers, growing out of the strike of 1873 and the Reading strike. In the strike of "'73" many of the Knights of Labor, or those who are now Knights, took the places vacated by Brotherhood men on the Pennsylvania lines. In the Reading strike of the Knights, members of the Brotherhood, in turn, supplanted them.

At the commencement of the "Q" strike, individual members of the Knights of Labor took it upon themselves to retaliate upon the Brotherhood, at least it was called retaliation, but the object was apparently to secure better jobs.

There is positive proof that these measures of

retaliation were not, in either case authorized by the heads of the organizations. The Burlington Company sought to make capital for themselves out of this old trouble, and did everything in their power to widen the breach.

During the months of January and February, the agents of the company thoroughly canvassed the labor districts of the East, searching out every dissatisfied Knight and every unprincipled character, who could by any possible means be induced to put the finishing touches to his disgrace. Among this horde were some few hitherto respectable workmen, who were induced by brilliant promises to drop their respectability and disgrace themselves by joining such a band and for such a cause. Retaliation was their excuse, but a thinner disguise never clothed a scoundrel. Had the Switchmen's Mutual Aid Association ever done them a wrong? And yet, more of these so-called Knights are switching cars to-day than are handling the throttle and scoop.

For a time these men were actually thought to be Knights of Labor in good standing, and coming West with the full sanction of their Order. Ample proof, however, exists that they were but the riffraff of the Order. It is but justice to the Knights of Labor to say that these fellows were a class who acknowledged allegiance to no particular Order, and recognized no authority. Many of them belonged to suspended Assemblies, or were expelled from the K. of L. as well as from the B. of L. E. for dissolute habits and other causes.

T. V. POWDERLY.

On February 29, Grand Master Workman Powderly, issued a noted letter to his Order, calling upon them to stand back and keep hands off in this strike. The following extract from the letter demonstrates the fact that Mr. Powderly's attitude was consistent with justice and right. "Let the past be forgotten in this strike; no matter how bitter you may feel toward these men, remember that they have not yet stepped out of the rut of selfishness, and it is best to teach them what manhood means by keeping your hands off the C., B. & Q. strike. The spectacle presented by men of labor who belong to different organizations rushing at each other's throats whenever a strike takes place, must be a gratifying thing to the employers of labor. It must indeed give satisfaction to the corporations to know that neither Knights of Labor nor Brotherhood men dare in future ask for better treatment, with any assurance of receiving it. It must be a consoling thought to the monopolist to know that his power is not half so dangerous to the labor organizations as the possibility that another labor organization will espouse his cause through revenge. Labor will forever be bound hand and foot at the feet of capital as long as one workingman can be pitted against another.

"No strike should be entered into until the court of last resort has been reached; until the last effort consistent with manhood has been made; until the heads of the opposing forces on both sides have been consulted, and their verdict given; until the last bridge has been burned between them; then, if it was determined that the last thing possible had been done to avert trouble, every detachment of labor's army—horse, foot and artillery—should be wheeled into line to defend the rights of men in the breach. Knights of Labor, from Maine to California, stand back! Keep your hands off! Let the law of retaliation be disregarded, and let the men of the "Q" road win this strike if they can!"

That all of these men did not stand back is not the fault of this organization. Bad men exist in every Order, and probably always will. The "Q" retain many of them, but it is no disgrace to the Knights of Labor. They are men who have not the principles of Knighthood in their hearts.

About the middle of April a committee of Brotherhood men went East to confer with Grand Master Workman Powderly. The result of that meeting was that all Knights of Labor who still acknowledged allegiance to that Order should be called off from all lines operated by the Burlington Company where they had taken the places of strikers. The general result of this order was not very satisfactory. As before stated, they were a class of men who recognized no authority from any labor organization.

The following circular of a later date gives the true standing of the Knights of Labor on this question:

OFFICE OF STATE MASTER WORKMAN, }
Beatrice, Neb.. June 21, 1888. }

AN APPEAL.

I have given thorough and conscientious examination into the troubles existing between the striking Brotherhood of Engineers, Firemen and Switchmen and the Chicago, Bur-

lington & Quincy Railroad Company. The justice of their
cause against this corporation appeals to my judgment and
my sympathies. It should arouse every Knight of Labor in
the State, and place him to the front in defense of their
cause and in placing opprobrium upon the Burlington monopoly. The Order should take a distinctive and pronounced
stand for these men, who are simply battling for justice, and
no more. What is the purpose of the C., B. & Q. people in
this struggle with the Brotherhood? It is to stamp organized
labor with defeat, and millions of dollars are behind them to
accomplish this result. Should they succeed, every laborer
and producer will sink lower in the scale of manhood and
deeper into the degradation of slavery. It is the purpose of
the C., B. & Q. to fasten perpetual manacles upon them, from
which there can be no escape but in death. It means slavery for
all who toil, more appalling and horrible than the slavery of
the South, the fetters of which were broken by war.

I urge, therefore, upon every knight in the State to boycott this road that is the enemy of labor. Do not ride in its
cars. Drive your stock to some competing line, and do not
sell your grain where it will be shipped by them. Let the
boycott be absolute and complete so far as your patronage
goes. Have nothing to do with those who are in business and
employ this road in any capacity. Spend your dollars with
those who are the friends of organized labor. Persuade your
friends to adopt the same course.

There is only one debt that the Knights of Labor owe to
the C., B. & Q. road, and that is the infamy of their eternal
hate. Its hand has forever been raised against us. Whenever
its employes have come to our ranks, that was sufficient ground
for their discharge from its service. Its power, its wealth, its
secret detective service and all the means at its command
have been aimed at our destruction. Do not stop to consider
that there have been differences in the past between the
Knights of Labor and the Brotherhoods. It is not the time to
argue which organization has been in the wrong. The past is
a dead thing; let us give our thoughts to the future and the
living present.

The question is, are we going to help this corporation to
destroy labor organizations, or are we going to present a solid
front, a phalanx of determined men, who will say to the Brother-

5

hoods, "We will stand by you till you conquer in this fight, and all the power of our membership and assemblies will be directed to help you win."

This is my theory of true knighthood, and I want to see it placed in successful practice in the present grave emergency.

Let us do more than this. Let us make certain the defeat of this corporation as a lasting memorial that will bear a lesson to all corporations so long as time shall be.

Fraternally,

M. D. HUBBARD, S. M. W.

STATE RAILWAY COMMISSION.

This book would be incomplete did it not give an extract of the testimony taken before the State Board of Warehouse and Railway Commissioners on the 3d, 4th and 5th days of April, 1888. This testimony grew out of the charges made before the Board by the citizens of Aurora. We are indebted to the *Sunday World* of April 15 for the matter herein contained, which was not published or referred to by any other Chicago paper, and was suppressed by the Board.

Citizens of Aurora vs. *The C., B. & Q. Railway Company:*

Testimony taken before the Board of Warehouse and Railway Commissioners of Illinois, on the 3d, 4th and 5th days of April, A. D. 1888:

Present: Alexander Sullivan, Esq., on behalf of the citizens of Aurora; Chester A. Dawes, Esq., on behalf of the C., B. & Q. Railway Company.

Franklin L. Bliss, a witness called on behalf of the complainants, having been duly sworn, was examined in chief by Mr. Sullivan, and testified as follows:

Q. What is your name? A. Franklin L. Bliss.

Where do you live? Rock Island, Illinois.

What is your occupation? Locomotive engineer.

In what company's employ are you? Chicago, Milwaukee & St. Paul.

How long have you been a locomotive engineer? Over twenty-three years.

Were you the engineer on the train on the Milwaukee road with which a Quincy train collided on February 27? I was.

State to the Board, as briefly as you can, the circumstances; what you did at that crossing; what it was your duty to do as to stopping and giving signals, and whether or not you performed your duty, and then state the occurrence of the accident? When I was within half a mile of this crossing I gave a long signal for the crossing; I brought the train to a full stop within 400 feet of the railroad crossing; then I stepped over and looked on the left side of the engine, and could see no train or hear no train on the left; on the right there was no train I could see; then I gave two whistles and started my train for the crossing; when I got the engine onto the crossing (the cab was about on the crossing) I looked to the left and saw a train coming down the Burlington track right at me.

Commissioner Marsh: Just after you got on the crossing? A. Yes; the cab of the engine was about on the crossing when I saw.

Commissioner Rinaker: Was there anything to hinder you seeing that train before you got onto the crossing?

Commissioner Marsh: Any obstruction in the way? A. Well there is a cut on the east. I should think the mouth of the cut was some 900 feet from the crossing on the Burlington road.

Mr. Sullivan: When you looked before you started your engine was there anything between you and that crossing—was the engine in sight? A. No, sir.

Q. Describe the grade on the Quincy road between that cut and where the collision occurred at the crossing; is it smooth? It is down-grade to the crossing.

From the mouth of the cut? Yes, sir.

To the crossing? Yes, sir.

Did that engine, after it came out of that cut, stop before it reached the crossing and collided with your train? A. No, sir.

It did not? No, sir. I gave two short whistles before I started the train, after making the stop.

You came to a full stop? I came to a full stop; yes, sir.

Commissioner Rogers: What crossing do you have reference to—the crossing at Aurora? A. This crossing is just about two miles and a quarter south of Fulton Junction, on the Milwaukee road.

Q. Where the C., B. & Q. crosses? A. Yes, sir.

Commissioner Rinaker: How near to the crossing were you when you stopped? Within 400 feet; the cylinder of my engine was just about opposite the stopping board.

Q. Go on and describe the accident. You were describing what you did, the signals you gave; go on and finish that. A. That was all the signals I did give.

Two sharp whistles? Yes; then I started the train. I didn't see the train till the engine got on the crossing, just about the cab. The "Q" engine struck my tender just about midway of the back truck.

Mr. Sullivan: What damage, if you know, was done to your train, and to the other, and what injuries to persons?

Commissioner Rinaker: The back truck of your engine or tender? A. Of the tender—it throwed my tender or the tank down into the ditch; took the back truck with it, and throwed the mail car also down the bank; wrecked the mail car, too; also the "Q" engine went off the track, and run along; the engine and baggage car kind of went over, nearly onto one side; went into the ground and stopped.

Q. Was yours a passenger train? A. Yes, sir.

Was the other the "Q"? Yes, sir.

Both passenger trains? Yes, sir.

Who, if anyone, was hurt on your train? There was a route agent by the name of Wilhelm; I don't know exactly what his name was.

Where does he live, do you know? Rock Island, I think. An express messenger by the name of Morrison.

Do you know where he lived? I do not.

Who else? A mail agent by the name of Brown.

Do you know whether or not anyone was hurt on their train—the Quincy train? The roadmaster, engineer and conductor of the train.

That was all that was injured? That was all that was injured.

Do you know their names? I do not.

F. L. Bliss, being recalled, was examined by Mr. Sullivan, and testified as follows:

Q. At what rate of speed did you pull out after you left

that 400-foot board—between that and the crossing? A. I pulled out slow; it would not average over about six or eight miles an hour, anyway.

Were you trying to make up for your lost time? No, sir.

Why? We have an order not to make up any time from Fulton Junction to three miles west of Albany. There was an order on the board, and has been there.

So that you were not trying to make up time, and were not running at an extraordinary rate of speed? Not running any faster than though we had been right on time.

And you think the time you were running between that 400 feet and the crossing was about six to eight miles? I don't think when we was on the crossing—I don't think it was over eight miles an hour, anyway—six or eight.

Mr. Dawes: You rely on your fireman, don't you, to look out for his side? A. No, sir.

Who do you rely on? I hardly ever go over the crossing without looking myself; still, he tells me, but I think it is safer to look myself.

You looked on your side? I did.

Did you look out on the other side? I did.

Where did you look out last? Before I started.

Before you started from the 400-foot post? Yes, sir.

Did you look out after that at all? Not after I started on the train until I got on the crossing.

The fireman was shoveling in coal, wasn't he—firing up? Yes, sir.

Did you look out of your side of the cab after you left the 400-foot station, down the Burlington track? Yes, sir; I looked on my side.

How long has that 400-foot post been there, do you know? The 400-foot on our track?

Yes. It has been there ever since I have run down there. I have been running about fourteen years on that run. I don't know how much longer it has been there.

Mr. Sullivan: That is all. The people that have been injured we could not get.

Mr. Dawes: We will admit people were injured. The engineer we shall call was injured more than anybody else.

D. W. Rhodes, a witness called on behalf of the Chicago, Burlington & Quincy Railroad Company, being first duly sworn, was examined in chief by Mr. Dawes, and testified as follows:

Q. What is your full name? A. D. W. Rhodes.

What is your business? Superintendent of motive power on the C., B. & Q. road.

Are the engineers responsible to you? Through my assistants they are directly responsible to me.

But they are immediate employes of your department? They are immediate employes of my department.

Of which you are the head? Yes, sir.

Do you know Mr. Pearce? Yes, sir.

What is his business now, and what was it on the 19th day of March? Mr. Pearce is assistant engineer of tests in our labratory at Aurora.

Is he an engineer in the employ of the Burlington road now? He is not a locomotive engineer.

Was he ever, at any time, an engineer in the employ of the Burlington road? He was never examined as an engineer for the Burlington road.

You say he was not? No, sir; he was not.

Where was he sent? He was sent on this Clinton run, from Mendota to Clinton.

Do you know about what time that run is made? No, I do not.

Was anybody sent with him? He had a pilot, the road-master was his pilot.

The roadmaster of that section or division? Yes, sir. I am not very clear about what Mr. Pearce's crew was. I had to take an engine out myself that morning, and I was not at Aurora.

Mr. Sullivan: Do you know anything about it at all, except from hearsay? Do you know from your own knowledge who was on the train? A. From being present, no.

Mr. Sullivan: This testimony on that subject should be stricken out. The witness: May I make one correction? I said I took an engine out myself that morning; I fired an engine out that morning.

Cross-examination by Mr. Sullivan:

Q. Did Mr. Pearce ever run a locomotive engine before? A. Mr. Pearce had handled a locomotive engine; yes, sir.

The question was, did he ever run a locomotive engine

before? Please answer that? I am not able to say whether he did or not.

Are you in the habit, when exercising your best judgment to select engineers, to put a man on the road to run a locomotive engine when you don't know whether he has ever run one before or not? In a case like this, where our trains were——

In any case? We do so; I would do so again.

Where the lives of the public and the property of the public are in peril, you will take a man without knowing whether he ever ran an engine before or not, and put him in charge of an engine? No, sir; Mr. Pearce's education and training justified me in believing that he could handle that train properly.

Do you believe any technical education in the shops, without practical experience, fits a man to be placed in charge of an engine to which is attached a passenger train? Properly guided by a pilot and conductor on the engine, I say so, decidedly.

You would do so at any time? If there had been no strike, you would select a man of that experience, would you? I would only do that under the circumstances as we were.

Only under emergencies? Yes, sir.

You would not say generally it is a wise thing for a railroad to do; would you? I would say under circumstances such as we were left in there it was a wise thing for us to do.

I ask you generally? If I had time to make a thorough examination of a man I certainly would do it.

William H. Pearce, a witness called on behalf of the C., B. & Q. railroad company, being first duly sworn, was examined in chief by Mr. Dawes, and testified as follows:

Q. What is your name? A. William H. Pearce.

What is your business? Assistant engineer of tests in the C., B. & Q.

State under what circumstances you to k this engine on the 27th day of February last? Upon learning of the strike, I, with several other young men, signed a letter to Mr. Rhodes offering to go out in any position which they should deem it advisable. I was detailed by the Master Mechanic to go to Mendota and take that train to Fulton, with the understanding that I was to have a pilot; we struck the train; we had as pilot the roadmaster. We left Mendota five minutes late, and we were about six minutes late when I first see the St. Paul train.

How far was that out of Mendota, do you remember? It was somewhere about in the neighborhood of sixty miles.

You had lost a minute in sixty miles, had you? Lost a minute in running sixty miles.

Who were with you on the engine beside the road-master? When we started out of Mendota there was only Mr. Chapin, the civil engineer of the Chicago Division, and the roadmaster, Mr. Seegers, and a machinist who came from the Aurora shop. After leaving Garden Plain, which is the last stop before arriving at the crossing, the conductor also came on the engine.

Were you familiar with that division, had you ever run over it before? No, I never knew it; I never run over it at all.

Now state, Mr. Pearce, how this accident occurred. We were going along, I should judge, about forty-five miles an hour. I will preface it by saying that the roadmaster was very careful all the way coming up, and I had no reason what-soever to fear any lack of duty in warning me of any such place; we were going about forty-five miles an hour, and I had to look out for my water; it was getting a little dark; we were going west; of course it cast a shadow and I could not see the water glass; after losing a little time that way I tried my gauge cocks; when I got through with that I looked up and I saw this St. Paul train; that is the first intimation I had of the crossing.

What did you do then? I shut off and put on the brakes.

Right off, did you? Yes, sir.

You struck this train as described? I struck a train; yes.

Did you do everything in your power to prevent that accident? Yes, sir; I don't see how I could do anything more.

Commissioner Rinaker: Tell exactly what you did do? A. I shut off and put the air on.

How far were you from the train, in your judgment, when you did that? I should say in the neighborhood of 600 feet when I saw it, and I would say right here about the speed, that that speed, down grade, would require about a thousand feet to stop; it has been proved by the Burlington tests.

Mr. Dawes: What became of you, do you know? A. I only know that from hearsay. I know I was knocked off the engine and they got me up; I was leaning against the drivers, they told me, laying up against the drivers; the engine jumped the track, I understand; I don't know; I didn't remember anything until the next morning.

Is your sight good—your eyesight? Yes; I think my sight is normal, with my glasses.

You can see at a distance, can you, as well as ordinary individuals? I think so.

In reference to your hearing? Well, I am hard of hearing in a room, but I am not hard of hearing on an engine.

Had you received any warning before coming to this crossing, as far as you remember of it? No.

It is fair to say that the roadmaster says he warned you; I say that in justification of him. He says he did.

You did not hear any notice; that is what you swear, isn't it? I did not hear him.

Are you, in your own judgment, from your education and experience, both in study and on the road, capable of running a locomotive engine? On such a train as that, yes; it is a branch road, and there are comparatively few trains; I would not care about going on a main line.

Cross-examination by Mr. Sullivan: Who was the pilot who was furnished you? A Mr. Seegers, the roadmaster.

Can you not hear without putting your hand up? I don't wish to be offensive, but I want, as a matter of fact, to find out. Not in that tone. I can hear, yes; but I can hear better by putting it up, as anyone could reasonably argue; probably you can yourself. It is not necessary to do that where there is any noise or confusion going on.

· Could you have heard a notice to stop, or a notice that there was a crossing, if Seegers had given it to you? I would have heard as well as any other person.

Then you would have heard him if he gave such an order or gave such information? You are very well aware of the fact you have to speak more or less loud on an engine to anyone.

Did anyone speak more or less loud to you as to notify you that there was a crossing there, and that you should stop 400 feet from it? No.

Did you notice the crossing board on the Quincy road? I did not.

There is a board 400 feet from that crossing, four or five feet in height?

Mr. Dawes: Who says there is a board there?

Mr. Sullivan: I will show there is by another witness.

Mr. Dawes: There may be, but I have not heard anybody say so yet.

Mr. Sullivan: How long would it have taken you to bring that train to a full stop, running at the rate of forty-five miles an hour? When I say how long, I mean in distance; at what space from that crossing should you have attempted to bring it to a full stop in order to stop it? A. If I knew the crossing?

How long would it take a train to stop? It would take in the neighborhood of 1,000 feet.

You could not have stopped it at the rate of speed you were running if you had noticed it at the 400 feet distance? No, sir.

When you got out of the cut was any information given to you that it was necessary to stop there? I received no information. The first intimation I had was the sight of the train.

Mr. Sullivan: Was there an engineer on the cab with you at the time? Yes, sir.

Wasn't that engineer who was on the cab at that time held responsible for it? He was.

When you were held responsible for it you never in your life run an engine that length before, did you? No, sir.

If you had been working at the engine-house, and there was no such emergency as this, would you have considered yourself competent to do it? Not on a road in which I was entirely unfamiliar.

You were entirely unfamiliar with this, were you not? I was entirely unfamiliar.

Did you shut off steam before you saw the Milwaukee train? No, sir.

How far was it from you when you did shut off the steam? Fifty or sixty feet.

Did you reverse the engine? No, sir, I did not. With a well designed driver-brake there is no benefit in reversing the engine.

Did you bring the lever down in front ? No, sir.

Did you drop the reverse lever forward when you shut off? I don't remember that particularly.

When you put the air on, did you use all that was indicated on your gauge? I naturally should do so.

Did you? No, I slapped the air around, put the handle full around; I didn't stop to see what was indicated on the gauge.

Did you use any sand? No.

Were quite excited at the time? I suppose I naturally was.

You lost your head in fact; isn't that the fact now? No, because it is still on my shoulders.

You might as well have been without a head; you lost your judgment, didn't you? I don't see that any judgment would come in after having shut the steam off and put the air on.

Couldn't you have used sand? I did not.

You could have used it if you had thought of it? No, sir; because I didn't see any benefit; as long as the drivers don't slip it is all right.

Do you know that sand will help to stop a train quicker? No, sir I don't know it.

Do you swear it will not? No, sir, because I have never made any experiment in that.

Then you know nothing about it? You don't know whether it would help or not? I have only my judgment, which is formed after quite an elaborate series of experiments on the brakes.

John F. Laughlin was examined in chief by Mr. Sullivan, and testified:

Q. What is your name? A. John Francis Laughlin.

Where do you live? At 818 Washtenaw avenue.

What is your business? Switchman, in charge of switch engine.

For what road are you working? Chicago, Burlington & Quincy; I was at one time, until I quit.

Were you employed on the 23d of March for that road? Yes, sir.

Why did you quit? Because I did not see fit to work with incompetent engineers.

What were you engaged at on the evening of March 23d, and where were you employed? March 23d I did not do much. I only took one train to the Stock Yards and came back. This accident I have reference to happened March 22d, I believe, at 10:30 p. m.

What were you doing on the evening of the 22d, and where were you employed? On the evening of the 22d of March I had fifty cars shoving into the new yard at Hawthorne, which is about three miles and a half, as near as I can judge, from Western avenue. We stopped to give me a chance to raise the semaphore for the protection of trains coming east, and also set the switches going into the new yard. I got up and gave the signal to go ahead, and as I did a crash came.

What character of train was it that run into yours—a freight? A freight train.

What was the condition of the track, so far as obstructions were concerned, between your train and the train which collided with you? There was no obstruction whatever; there was a clear view four miles or three miles and a half; something like that.

What time in the evening was it? About half-past ten.

Had you a headlight on your engine? Yes, sir.

Had you a light on the other end of your train? No, sir; only my own lamp.

You were at that end? And a red light; yes, sir.

You had a red light, as well? Yes, sir.

Do you know the number of the engine which collided with yours? Yes, sir; 310.

What was the number of yours? 176.

Was engine 310 flagged? I presume it was, according to my helpers' statement.

Your helpers are here, are they? Yes, sir.

You had enough helpers to give the necessary flagging? I believe I had; I had two.

To how many of these new men did you give signals who were unable to answer or failed to answer the signals? I should say three or four.

Did you have any conversation with any of them in relation to the signals? No, sir; well, I had a conversation with one; I gave him a signal and he says, "I don't understand that signal."

Was that signal which you gave him and which he said he did not understand the usual signal given by railroad men? Yes, sir.

The same signal which has been used on the road all the time you have been in its employ? Yes, sir.

When was that, about what time? That was a couple or three nights before I left.

Commissioner Marsh: State what conversation between you and him there at the time he told you he did not understand that signal? I merely gave him a signal to back up. He says, "Partner, I don't understand that signal." I merely says to him, "What kind do you understand—steamboat signals?" He says, "No, stationary engines."

William G. Frisbie was examined by Mr. Sullivan and testified:

Q. Were you on the train to which engine 176 was attached? A. I belonged to that crew.

At Hawthorne, March 22   I belonged to that crew? Yes, sir.

Did you flag 310 that night? I did.

State to the Commissioners how far you went from your own engine, 176, to flag 310, the one which collided with it? I can tell you perhaps better by car lengths; I can make a guess at the number of feet. I did not measure it exactly. I should think it was in the neighborhood of 1,500 feet to 2,000 feet that I was back of where our engine stood. I found the train was not coming to a stop, and kept going back myself as long as it was possible, giving them all the swing that it was proper and right to stop him. He paid not the slightest attention to my signal; never even whistled for brakes until after his train passed me.

Did you start back as soon as your train stopped to flag? Yes, sir.

You went as far as you could? Yes, sir.

Re-direct examination by Mr. Sullivan:

Q. Did you ever, in all your experience, know a case

where an engineer was flagged on a clear track, as in this case, and disobeyed a signal and run into another train? No, sir.

Stewart W. Hadlock, examined in chief by Mr. Sullivan, testified as follows:

Q. What is your name ? A. Stewart W. Hadlock.

Where do you reside? At Aurora.

What is your business? Engineer.

How long have you been an engineer? Nineteen years.

In what company's employ were you recently? C., B. & Q.

How long were you in the employ of that company? Twenty-three years.

As engineer and fireman? Engineer and fireman both.

Do you know Hose De Witt? I do.

Do you know in whose employ he now is? He is in the employ of the C., B. & Q.

In what capacity? Passenger engineer.

Hector H. Hall was examined in chief by Mr. Sullivan, and testified:

Q. What is your name? A. Hector H. Hall.

Where do you live? At Pullman.

What is your occupation? Engineer.

What company are you working for? Pullman Company.

Do you know Hose De Witt? Yes, sir.

How long have you known him? About eight years.

Is he a sober man? No, sir.

What is his general reputation for sobriety? He is an habitual drunkard.

Is that the reputation in the neighborhood where he lives? Yes, sir.

Have you ever heard it discussed? His wife has been around to all the saloons forbidding them to sell him anything.

Why? Because he was an habitual drunkard.

When did you see him last? I think it was last Thanksgiving day.

What condition was he in then? He was very drunk.

Did you ever see him sober? Well, no, sir; very seldom. I have once or twice, probably; as a general thing he was under the influence of liquor.

John B Clark, examined in chief by Mr. Sullivan, testified:

Q. State your name? A. John B. Clark.

Where do you live? Aurora.

What is your business? I was a locomotive engineer.

How long were you engaged in that capacity? Ten years, probably.

For what company were you employed? Chicago, Burlington & Quincy.

Did you serve on any committee for that road while you were in its employ? I was on the local examining board for the Chicago division.

Do you know Hose De Witt? I do.

How long have you known him? About fourteen years, I think.

Do you know he was discharged from this company because of his connection with a wreck at Naperville? I do.

Do you know what his reputation for sobriety is and has been during all the time of your acquaintance? He was always a hard drinker, when he fired and run here both.

Have you known him since he was in the employ of the company; have you seen him since? I have seen him on my way through Plano; he worked at Plano for the Plano Manufacturing Company, and I see him there about in the neighborhood of a year ago; he struck me for a ride to Chicago.

Mr. Dawes: I object to any specific instance of drunkenness a year ago.

Mr. Sullivan: Was he drunk or sober? A. He was not sober.

Did you ever see him sober? I don't think I did; not what I should call dead sober.

You have known him eight years? I have known him fourteen years.

Why did you refuse to give him a ride when he applied to you? Well, it was against the rules; and then he was too full of whisky to be a safe man to have around there.

You haven't seen him since, then? I have not, except since he came back to work for the C., B. & Q.

Acting as engineer? Yes, sir.

Passenger or freight? Passenger.

On what road? On the C., B. & Q., on the main line?

Mr. Dawes, cross-examining: Did you regard that as a proper method of determining the qualifications of engineers? A. Yes, sir; it is well enough.

. Is this (handing witness a paper) an accurate copy of the protest of the Brotherhood? I will direct your attention to Article 22. I don't represent the Brotherhood; I am here as a witness.

I will ask you whether you know as a matter of fact, Mr. Clark, whether Article 22 is a copy of a grievance presented by the Brotherhood of Locomotive Engineers to the Burlington road? I did not present it.

I understand you did not; you know, do you not?

Mr. Sullivan: I object to all this as immaterial.

Commissioner Rinaker: I do not regard that as cross-examination at present. Is that offered for the purpose of showing that the rule itself was not regarded as a proper one?

Mr. Dawes: I want to ask this witness what his opinion is of this particular grievance.

Mr. Sullivan: How often have you seen him in eight years? A. He laid around Aurora two or three years before he got a job any place.

He lived around Aurora two or three years after he was discharged? Yes, sir.

When he hung around Aurora for two or three years did you see him regularly? He hung around a variety saloon that used to be there in Aurora.

Commissioner Rinaker: How often do you mean we shall understand you are stating you have seen this man drunk in the last eight or ten years?

Commissioner Rogers: When was it he wanted to come up with you on the engine? A. As near as I can remember it was in the neighborhood of a year ago.

Commissioner Rinaker: How many times have you seen him drunk? A. He was drunk at that time.

How many more times? Between the seven years before that? Well, I would not want to say how many times; but at the time he was hanging around Aurora he was off and on. He would go away and hunt for a job and come back, go away and come back; that is the way he was.

Was he drunk when you would see him around this variety show? Yes, we very seldom seen him sober.

Mr. Sullivan: Prior to this controversy between the railroad and its employes could such a man as De Witt receive employment as an engineer; would you have employed such a man?

(Objected to by Mr. Dawes.)

Q. Would they employ a man who had been dismissed as being responsible for a wreck, as this man was?

(Objected to by Mr. Dawes.)

Commissioner Rinaker: Do you know why he was discharged? A. He was discharged for having a collision about half a mile east of Naperville station.

You know that from your own knowledge? Yes; I was mixed up a little bit in it myself. I came near getting into trouble with it myself.

Hector H. Hall being recalled, was examined by Commissioner Rogers, and testified as follows:

Q. How long is it since this notice was given by De Witt's wife to the saloon-keepers not to give him liquor? A. I think it was on Thanksgiving day, or the day after.

That is last year? Yes, sir.

That was on Thanksgiving day? Thanksgiving day or the day after; I am not positive which.

J. A. Murray, locomotive engineer of thirteen years' service, residing at Rock Island, testified that Frank Hamilton, Frank Horn, Joseph Roach, J. Logston, Harry Zimmerman and William Patterson, running engines on the C., B. & Q. R. R., were brakemen, conductors and baggagemen, respectively; that he was acquainted with them all for eight to ten years, and that they were inexperienced as engineers or firemen.

Frank Hamilton, witness on behalf of the C., B. & Q. Railroad Company, testified:

Q. Give your name in full? A. Frank Hamilton.

What is your business? Formerly conductor until the 10th of last month; now I am running an engine.

Conductor on the C., B. & Q.? Yes, sir; St. Louis division.

How long have you been a railroad man? For the C., B. & Q. Company, running a train since November, 1880, with the exception of five months, up until the 10th of last month.

Have you been examined as to the manipulation of an engine? To a certain extent.

By whom? Mr. Wallace.

Is Mr. Wallace here? Mr. Wallace is here.

6

Cross-examination by Mr. Sullivan:

Q. You never got any technical instruction as to the running of an engine in your life, did you? A. Explain that word, please.

You never got any instruction in the shop from those who manufacture engines and are familiar with their detail? No, sir.

You don't understand the meaning of the word technical yourself? I do; yes, sir.

Why do you want me to explain it? Because I wanted to understand.

Witness testified that he had been handling engines off and on ever since he had been on the road.

Q. What you mean is you jumped on; would go on when the regular engineer in charge was there? A. Yes, sir.

And the fireman in charge was there? I run the engine a certain distance.

You were allowed to handle it in their presence, just as many others are allowed? Yes, sir.

Do you mean to tell this Commission, on your oath, that in that way you acquired sufficient knowledge to make you a competent engineer? That is the way, from what I understand, to learn to be an engineer. The way they all get to be engineers.

You say you were examined to some extent. Were you not examined as thoroughly as all other men were examined? I don't know how other men were examined.

How did you come to say you were examined to some extent? What do you mean by that? I mean to the extent that I was able to answer the questions.

You were only examined to that extent you were able to answer, and you were not examined as to those you were not able to answer? I don't know if there were any questions I was not to answer or not; I answered all the questions.

You used that expression, you were examined to some extent. I want to know what you mean by that? I answered all the questions that were asked me.

Do you mean to say that all questions were asked you which are equally asked applicants for employment as engineers? I do not.

Was anyone else examined at the same time you were? There was not.

Who was present when you were being examined? Anyone but the Board? No; there was not.

No one but the Board of Examiners? No.

Where were you examined? The principal place was in the building where the general officers are.

Were you examined more than once? I was instructed another time.

I asked you about examinations? No, sir; not on an engine.

How long did your examination take? I could not tell that.

How many questions were you asked? I could not say; I did not count them.

Have you no idea without counting them? I answered more questions—I asked and answered more questions than was asked me.

You examined yourself, practically, did you? The Board was there to hear it.

The Board was there to hear you examine yourself—asking questions and answering them? Those I did not thoroughly understand were questions I asked, and then I answered my way, and if I was not right, then I was instructed.

And upon that instruction which you got at that time you were employed as an engineer on the road? Oh, no; this is since.

How long after that was it before you were put in charge of an engine, since you got this instruction? I took an engine on the 10th of last month, and I run up to yesterday.

When was your examination? To-day.

You were examined to-day? Yes, sir.

Was this the first examination that took place? This is the first.

You were not examined before you were put in charge of an engine? No, sir.

You were put in charge of an engine without an examination at all? Without any examination.

You were this morning examined, and prepared for being examined here; is that it? No, sir; I don't know as I was prepared at all. I asked questions, and they were answered to me. If I could explain them in the language that was used in regard to the management of engines.

And that is the first time you have been examined by anybody representing this road as an engineer? Examined on an engine.

Did you ever draw pay as an engineer or as a fireman at any time in the employ of this or any other railroad company in the United States before this? As an engineer or fireman?

As an engineer or fireman? I did not.

Did you ever perform the duties of an engineer or fireman at any time in your life before this date, on any road? That is, to draw pay for it?

To draw pay for it, and perform its duties regularly? No, sir.

Did you ever put a wick in a headlight? I did.

When? The other day.

Not until that? That is the first one, but I have frequently saw it done.

How old are you? I was thirty-four years old on the 16th day of last January.

Can you tell what the notches in the quadrant are for? Yes, sir.

Please do so? They are to govern the working of an engine.

State in what respect they govern the working of an engine? They start from the center and work both ways; the forward and back motions drop the engine down forward and you give her the full stroke. If you put her back to a less stroke and increase the speed.

What do you mean by the stroke? The stroke of the piston that travels in the cylinder.

What is the stroke of your engine? I don't know.

Has an engine more or less stroke when it is hooked down or hooked up? It has the same stroke, but it receives steam through the ports to a less stroke.

In what condition? Both ways; either working in the forward or back motion.

What do you refer to when you speak of receiving more steam? Can you explain that? To a certain extent, yes.

To that certain extent please explain it? As the engine

is working you drop her down and give her full stroke and she is receiving steam at full stroke; as you cut her back she receives steam to a less portion as you cut her back, and then start to travel the other way—the valve it is.

Do you know anything about the points of cut-off of a valve on an engine? No, sir.

You never got any instruction on that subject? No, sir.

You were not examined on it this morning, were you? No, sir.

Evidence of a large number of expert engineers and practical railroad men was heard, together with the testimony of the incompetent men. A copy of the entire proceedings is in the hands of Mr. Alexander Sullivan, counsel for the Brotherhood.

INTER-STATE COMMERCE COMMISSION.

The result of the State Board's examination, with a vast amount of new evidence, was prepared to place before the Inter-State Commerce Commission, which had signified its willingness to sit in Chicago May 1, to examine into the charges that the Burlington was operating its lines with incompetent men. For some reason never made public the promised investigation was not made. The Brotherhood side of the case was ready, and in the hands of experienced legal counsel; however, no action was taken by the Commission.

MEETING OF THE STOCKHOLDERS.

As the stockholders were to meet on May 16, it was expected that they, having suffered great financial loss from the strike, would take some steps toward bringing about a settlement between the men and the company. It was considered by the strikers that the

road had not been successfuly operated by the class of
men then in its employ, and that self-interest would
prompt the stockholders to do justice to their old employes.

Contrary to the anticipations of the men, the
management was unanimously endorsed at this meeting and by this action gave notice that nothing in the
line of concessions could be expected.

FINAL ACTION OF THE MEN.

Subsequent to this meeting, the Joint Grievance
Committee was convened, and it was resolved not to
declare the strike off but to continue resistance indef-
initely, this action to be subject to the approval of
the men. The resolution of the Committee was duly
submitted to the men along the line, and a vote was
taken as to whether the strike should be declared off
or not. The result of the vote was an almost unanimous expression to continue the strike without abate-
ment.

After the stockholders' meeting, the men at Chicago appointed a day to discuss anew the proposition
to declare the strike off. This caused great uneasi-
ness along the line, but was only done in order to
give those who had not been present at the first vote
taken an opportunity to express their sentiments.
This discussion, like the preceding one, ended in an
unanimous decision to continue the strike.

Every effort had been made by the company to break
the lines. At Galesburg and other points, it was claimed
that large sums of money had been offered to individ-

uals to break the ranks and again enter the services
of the company. Outside of Chicago, the men were
subject to all manner of persecutions to compel them
to yield to the company's offers, but without effect;
not a single case of weakness was developed after the
second week of the strike.

In Chicago, as before stated, but two men returned, one of these, a yardmaster, had been struggling under the name of "scab" since "'82" and he was
naturally expected to take the course that he did.
On the morning of March 23, he was the first yardmaster to refuse to do duty as a switchman, and the
first and only one to seek reinstatement. At other
points along the line, the record is even better than
this. Probably not over a dozen men weakened; from
Chicago to Denver, all have stood firm and solid on
the ground they first occupied.

The following quotation from the Brotherhood
circular heretofore alluded to, will be of interest.

"THE LOYALTY OF THE STRIKERS.

"Just here it is proper to place upon record the fact
—luminous in the annals of labor strikes—of the loy-
alty of the men, their devotion to principle, and their
unexampled faithfulness to their obligations. As one
man they responded to the call. So thoroughly im-
bued were they with the justice of their cause, that with
an unanimity which will forever challenge the admiration of manly men, they surrendered their positions and
faced with an unaltering fortitude all the privations
incident to a strike, rather than sacrifice their manhood, their independence and self-respect.

"Be it said to the everlasting honor of the engineers, firemen and switchmen on the C., B. & Q. system, that they acted their part nobly from the first to the last. There was no deserters or traitors to the cause; faithful to their obligations, true to their manhood, honorable in all their methods, they have dignified themselves and glorified the Orders to which they belong, and while courage and fidelity have admirers, they will be remembered for their unyielding purpose by every true knight of the throttle and scoop whereever the iron horse draws a train."

FINANCIAL CONDITION OF THE ROAD.

In June the following statement appeared in the Chicago *Herald:* "The Burlington Company is having a hard time to make both ends meet. Its statement of net earnings for the month of May, which came to light yesterday, showed a decrease of $803,000, and for the first five months of 1888 the loss compared with the corresponding period last year reaches the astounding total of $4,194,172. Never in the history of Western railroads has such a disastrous record been made by a big railway corporation in so short a time. Less than a year ago the Burlington Company was reported to be the strongest corporation of its kind in the country. It paid the highest rate of dividends, and its securities commanded larger prices than any similar paper on the New York Stock Exchange. Since the beginning of 1888 its dividend rate has been reduced from eight to four per cent, and even the four per cent has not been earned by many thousand dollars. The interest requirements, which come ahead of the stock, alone amount to, approximately, $6,000,-000 per year, or at the rate of $500,000 per month. The net earnings for five months, however, are only a little over $1,000,000, or less than half of what would be required to pay current interest charges. In face of this showing, however, the company has, since the beginning of 1888, paid three per cent in dividends on $77,000,000 stock. This required an expenditure of nearly $2,400,000. If this $2,400,-000 be deducted from the net earnings of the company for the first five months of the year an actual deficit of nearly $1,400,000 is left, without allowing anything whatever for interest on bonds, which are always a prior lien. Deducting $2,500,000 interest charges, which somebody must pay, and the deficit is swelled to nearly $4,000,000. To put the matter plainly, the Burlington Company lacks $4,000,000 of being able to pay its debts out of its current earnings. It had a a surplus at the end of last year of $1,000,000, but this has been wiped out, and a floating indebtness of approximately $3,000,000 now stares the Burlington management in the face. It is currently rumored that the company has been trying to negotiate a loan of $2,000,000 in Chicago to help it out of its present dif-ficulties, but these negotiations have fallen through, and it is understood that an effort will be made to raise the money in the East. The depreciation in value of the $77,000,000 stock, of at least one-third, is another serious loss, which will probably never be retrieved."

THE DYNAMITE PLOT.

July 5, J. A. Bowles, Thos. Broderick and J. Q. Wilson were arrested on the train leaving Aurora, at 2:15 P. M., by Deputy Marshal Burchard and Superintendent McGinty of the Pinkerton Agency. A package of some substance, said to be dynamite, was taken from the rack over the seat occupied by Wilson. They were arraigned before United States Commissioner Hoyne, under section 5353, United States Statutes, which provides a penalty of $1,000 to $10,000 fine for transporting or having in possession dynamite on trains or vessels carrying passengers.

Chairman Hoge was sent for, but when he learned the gravity of the charge against the prisoners he had little comfort to give them, but promised to secure an attorney if he found on investigation that their cause was worthy. All three of the men denied ownership of the package found in the rack. Bowles came to Aurora at the beginning of the strike, and ran an engine for thirteen days. His brother finally induced him to leave the service of the company, and he was taken into the Brotherhood Division at Aurora. The Burlington officials testified that Broderick was in their employ as late as April last, two months after the strike began. Wilson was a Pinkerton detective. Thus it will be seen that the trio were Burlington and Pinkerton employes.

The company claimed that dynamite was used at Eola, West Aurora, Galesburg and Creston, to blow up and wreck trains, but that no damage was done, except to a portion of a flange on an engine wheel at

Eola. In some of these cases a portion of the dynamite was found unexploded, together with parts of the
wrapper. If this stuff had really been dynamite, it is
impossible to conceive how part of the cartridge could
have remained unexploded.

J. A. Bauereisen, Chief of the Aurora Division of
B. of L. E., was arrested July 6 as an accomplice, it
having been claimed that Bowles received the package
from him before starting for Chicago with Wilson and
Broderick.

Alexander Smith was arrested July 6. Smith is
a fireman, and was charged with having handled the
dynamite in connection with the explosion at Eola and
West Aurora.

Attorneys Donohue and David were retained for
the defense of these men.

Chairman Hoge stated that the Brotherhood did
not tolerate violence of any kind, and would not come
to the assistance of any member caught in the act of
committing crime. The Brotherhood would look into
these cases, and if satisfied that the men were victims
of a conspiracy, it would aid and defend them, but if
it were shown that they had explosives and meant violence, they would be left to shift for themselves. At
this time Mr. Hoge was charged by the Burlington
people with having issued a circular April 16, to the
various divisions of the Brotherhood, advising that a
large number of engineers go to work for the road, and,
after disabling as many engines as possible with sal-
soda and emory, to quit in a body. Mr. Hoge denies
having written this circular, or of having signed it,

and stated that it was a forgery, if it existed at all.
However, Hoge and Chairman Murphy of the firemen
were arrested July 10 for conspiracy, and held under
the Merritt law in bonds of $1,500, which was furnished
by W. R. Fitzgerald. The complaint alleged that the
defendants issued a circular with the fraudulent or ma-
licious intent, wrongfully and wickedly to injure the
property of the Chicago, Burlington & Quincy railroad.
The penalty upon conviction is five years in the pen-
itentiary or a fine of $2,000, or both. The warrant
also contained the names of John J. Kelly and J. H.
McGilvery, secretaries to Hoge and Murphy, who were
arrested later in the day, but not locked up. Kelly
made a statement to the effect that he issued the circular at the dictation of Hoge, and that the latter
signed it. It was written with hektograph ink and
copied on a hektograph. Kelly also swore that he
had been in the employ of Pinkerton for several
months, during which time he acted as secretary to
Hoge. This man belonged to the Brotherhood of Firemen, but was running a switch engine on the "Q" in
in Chicago, and at the time of the strike was taken
into the Brotherhood of Engineers. He is a tall,
slender man of twenty-seven or twenty-eight years,
blonde, very natty in appearance, small brown mous-
tache, light eyes inclined to be deep set, and a clear
ringing voice, like the voice of a woman. He was
considered of a giddy, frothy nature by his intimates,
who were surprised at his ability to keep secret the
fact that he was in the employ of Pinkerton.

George Godding, an engineer, was arrested in

Aurora July 9, charged with Bauereisen in violating the United States law in handling dynamite.

George Clark, an engineer, was arrested at Galesburg July 17, charged with the same offense. During the examination of these men, Bowles, Smith, Wilson, Kelly and McGilvery appeared with the prosecution as detectives and informers.

Bauereisen was tried, and sentenced to two years imprisonment, at the last term of Kane County Court, at Geneva, Ill. He was convicted on the testimony of the informers and Pinkerton men, Bowles, Broderick, Smith and Wilson. The weight of evidence was clearly in favor of Bauereisen, but the fact that it was a Kane County jury, and that the Burlington Company was the prosecutor, settled the case against him. An appeal for a new trial is now pending.

None of the other cases have matured, and probably never will.

The general opinion of the strikers, and those who have been particularly interested in these cases, can be summed up in a few words. Knowing that the strike had financially wrecked the property, the managment found it necessary to make capital for themselves, and concluded that a dynamite scheme would answer their purpose.

They believed that the Brotherhoods were a law abiding class of citizens, and that they would be dumfounded at the evidence of a dynamite plot, and immediately declare the strike off. That it was originally intended as a bluff is proven by the low grade of dynamite used, which had scarcely the explosive power of black powder. The evidence shows that the "Q" employes and the detectives procured and used the stuff without effect. The only evidence against the Brotherhood men was that they had been told by these spies what they were doing; and while the defendants placed no reliance in the story, this knowledge was considered sufficient evidence of guilt to hold them as accomplices. This course was probably decided upon when it was found impossible to make them active participants in the crime.

In the case of Hoge and Murphy, the web was easier to weave. Having a Pinkerton man as Hoge's secretary, it was a simple matter to put up a fraudulent circular, and back it up with the utterances of other confederates who visited him, and sought to induce him to resort to violence as a means of compeling a settlement of the strike.

PROPOSITIONS FOR A SETTLEMENT.

July 14, Mr. Stone sent for Chairmen Hoge and Murphy to talk over a settlement of the strike. Being under bonds, Hoge and Murphy declined to go without their attorney; therefore, Mr. Alexander Sullivan was included in the invitation. They met Mr. Stone at his residence the same evening, but having no authority to make a settlement, only a general conversation ensued. Mr. Stone indicated a willingness to take up the schedule and pay as good wages as was paid by the other roads, especially so in the passenger runs. Another meeting was arranged for July 16, at which meeting Messrs. Arthur, Sargent, Sullivan, Hoge and

Murphy, on behalf of the men, and Messrs. Stone, Perkins and Dexter, for the company, were present. Mr. Perkins had arrived unexpectedly from Boston, and seemed dissatisfied with the action of Mr. Stone in calling the meeting, and for a time refused to make any concessions. Mr. Stone insisted, and the following was drawn up as a basis of settlement by the company:

"If the strike be declared off, the company agrees to take back such of the old men as can at present be given employment, and as business increases and more men are needed, they will be taken from the ranks of the strikers in preference to hiring men who had not previously been in the employ of the company.

"The company further agree that those men not so taken back would not be blacklisted, and that those whose previous record had been good would be given letters of recommendation. Mr. Perkins also agreed to rescind the order of J. D. Besler, dated March 25, to the effect that the switchmen would not again be employed by the Burlington company.

"That engineers, firemen and switchmen would be treated alike in the matter of re-employment."

This was in substance all that the company would concede. As these gentlemen had no authority to make any settlement without the consent of the men, it was decided to submit the proposition to them along the entire system, and Messrs. Hoge, Murphy and the writer were appointed to lay the matter before them. Mr. Arthur was opposed to the switchmen being represented on this committee.

Before going out on the road, a meeting of the Chicago strikers was held at Curran's Hall. In order to get the matter properly before them, the following resolution was put by the chairman, "*Resolved*, That the striking engineers, firemen and switchmen do hereby appoint the following Committee to settle the strike: Arthur, Sargent, Alexander Sullivan, Hoge, Murphy and Hall, with the understanding that we will abide by their decision and will accept the above proposition of the company, if no better terms can be obtained by the Committee." Arthur, Sargent and Mr. Sullivan strongly recommended the acceptance of the terms, and sent letters to that effect by the Committee to the men along the line.

The resolution was rejected by the Chicago men, and, in fact, by every body of strikers along the entire system. In these terms of settlement nothing was said about dismissing the dynamite cases, it being understood that they would be continued.

July 17 the Committee left Chicago to place the proposition before the men, and returned July 27. The strikers everywhere decided to accept no terms that did not include the signing of their schedule and the absolute discharge of all the new men. They considered that the company had asked them to make an unconditional surrender, and that the conspiracy cases had influenced their leaders to side with the company, and they would not now make any settlement that was not made by the entire Grievance Committee and include the whole schedule and discharge of the new men. Hoge and Murphy knew the temper of the men and knew what the result would be, but felt it their duty to present the propositions as instructed by their chiefs, Arthur and Sargent, and to give the men a complete statement of the condition of the strike, prospects of support, etc. It was a disagreeable duty, but they performed it faithfully. Many of the men were inclined to censure the Committee for presuming to offer them such terms.

UNION MEETING AT ST. JOE, JULY 24, 1888.

The following is the official report:

The Chairman stated the purpose of the meeting was to discuss the merits of the C., B. & Q. strike and to try and adopt some plan to bring it to a speedy termination. He also explained and outlined the situation of affairs on the C., B. & Q. R. R.

The Chairman then introduced Bro. G. W. Hitchens, Chairman of the G. G. Com., K. C., Ft. S. & G. R. R., who made a good speech, encouraging the C., B. & Q. Bros. and saying that he was in favor of the Boycott and Federation.

Bro. R. Powers, a member of the B. of R. B., was then introduced, and spoke encouragingly to the C., B. & Q. Bros., telling them to stand firm and they were sure to win.

Bro. F. P. Sargent, G. M. of the B. of L. F., was the next speaker. He was in favor of Federation, but did not speak very encouragingly to the C., B. & Q. Bros. in their struggle for Right and Justice.

Bro. Bailey, of the S. M. A. A., made an able address, which was enthusiastically received.

Bro. L. W. Rodgers, of the B. of R. B., and a man who has traveled over the C., B. & Q. R. R. several times, spoke and outlined the condition of the C., B. & Q., and urged the the Bros. to stand firm and they were sure of victory.

Speeches were made by Bro. Wm. McClain, of Quincy, and a member of the G. G. Com. of the C., B. & Q.; Bro. Slattery, of Butte City, M. T.; J. F. Bryan, of Creston, Iowa; and a great many other Bros. of the different organizations, who nearly all spoke in favor of Federation and said they would do all in their power to assist the C., B. & Q. Bros. who are now battling for justice. And they all told the Bros. to never declare the strike off but to fight it to the bitter end.

On motion, a committee of nine was appointed to draw up resolutions and adopt a line of action for this meeting.

The Chairman appointed the following Committee on Resolutions: W. H. Young, of Div. 307; W. F. Gould, Div. 184; R. Lacy, 105, B. of L. F.; T. J. Hayes, 44, B. of L. F.; L. W. Rodgers, B. of R. B.; T. Slattery, 151, B. of R. B.; F. Wells, Grand Lodge. S. M. A. A.; and T. C. Lyons, No. 9, S. M. A. A.

On motion adjourned until 9 o'clock, A. M., July 25, 1888.

Second Day.

Meeting called to order by F. P. McDonald in the chair.

On motion resolutions were ordered read, and each article taken up and adopted or rejected at one time.

The following resolutions were read and unanimously adopted, the last article being debated freely:

To the Engineers, Firemen, Switchmen and Brakemen, in Union Meeting assembled:

We, your Committee on Resolutions, beg leave to report the following:

Resolved, That in regard to the alleged dynamite plot, we denounce all unlawful acts; and that while we believe the accused innocent until proven guilty, yet should any member of our organization be proved guilty of the atrocities charged, we will not only promptly expel them, but be the first to demand their punishment.

Resolved, That we regard this as a conspiracy by the C., B. & Q. Co. and the Pinkertons, to bring our Order into disrepute, and turn public opinion and sympathy against us; and we ask the public to withhold their decision until the case has been passed upon by a fair and impartial jury.

Resolved, That we thank the managers of this meeting for their vigilance in discovering the company's spy who had been secreted in the opera house to report our proceedings, and that we denounce such dishonorable methods of obtaining information.

Resolved, That we, the engineers, firemen, switchmen and brakemen represented in this meeting, heartily endorse the plan of federation, and ask our coming conventions to authorize immediate action on this subject.

Resolved, That this meeting ask Bros. Hoge and Murphy, or the G. G. Com. of the C., B. & Q., to place on the payroll the names of the trainmen who struck April 1, 1888, and that they receive $40 per month for the time they have been out.

Resolved, That each and every delegate at this union meeting be instructed to use every endeavor to have his subordinate Division or Lodge, take such action as will guarantee financial support to our brothers now struggling for their legitimate rights, until such time as the several conventions shall convene, and shall incorporate in their constitutions such laws as shall thoroughly unite the several organizations.

Resolved, That we return to our respective Divisions and Lodges and notify our constituents to prepare to place a boycott on C., B. & Q. cars as soon as the Chairmen of the several Grievance Committees think it practicable, and we earnestly ask the Chairmen to institute this boycott as soon as in their judgment it can be worked with advantage to our cause.

Resolved, That this meeting heartly endorse the action taken by the C., B. & Q. Brothers, in refusing to declare the strike off.

All business pertaining to the purpose of the meeting being accomplished, the meeting adjourned at 5:15 P. M., July 25.

At a special meeting of the engineers at St. Joe, a plan was formed to call together the Chairmen of all the Grievance Committees in the United States and Canada authorized by the chiefs of the Brotherhoods to meet in St. Louis August 9, 1888.

The previous meeting at Kansas City, New York and St Joe were the results of local arrangements, and unauthorized by the chiefs of the Brotherhoods, and their actions were without proper authority, although giving expression to the general feelings of the men. A Committee was appointed to visit Chiefs Arthur and Sargent and request them to make an official call of all the Chairmen of Grievance Committees. This was done, and the meeting convened in St. Louis August 9.

SECRET MEETING AT ST. LOUIS.

Chiefs Arthur and Sargent were present. The entire Grievance Committee of the Burlington and the Chairmen of all the other Committees composed the assembly. All work was done in secret session. Nothing whatever was given to the public. The strike was the only question dealt with at this meeting. Many of the men favored an immediate boycott of "Q" cars and "Q" freight. After two days of discussion, it was agreed that the time and conditions were not such as to warrant a boycott; it was believed that the road had no business of consequence to be injured. This matter was then laid aside to be taken up in October. Another Committee was appointed to confer with the "Q" officials. This Committee was composed of Chairmen of roads not on strike.

The meeting adjourned Saturday, August 11. On Monday, August 13, Alexander Sullivan, Chairman Vrooman of the Union Pacific and his committee had an interview with Vice President Peasley and General Superintendent Besler.

The meeting was an informal one. The proposition presented by the Committee was a demand that all the men be taken back in a body; that the former proposition of Mr. Stone, to pay as good wages as his neighbors, be accepted by the Brotherhood. Mr. Peasley stated that he had no power to act in the absence of Manager Stone and President Perkins, but that he would submit the proposition to these officials on their return from the East. He also said that the company desired peace with the Brotherhoods.

No action was taken by Messrs. Stone and Perkins; the only result of the meeting was to strengthen them in their determination to fight the Brotherhoods to the end.

All efforts to produce a boycott had failed. The only result of the union meetings held at various points was to convince the strikers that the boycott was not necessary, in fact that they had already won the strike. They continued their meetings, and were just as much out of the way of the company as though they had been locked up for months. In the meantime, and in fact from the beginning of the strike, the company had been moving heaven and earth in their efforts to bring victory out of what seemed hopeless defeat. Starting with an inferior grade of men, they have been constantly weeding out the poorer ones as fast as a more competent man appeared who was willing to work for them. A very great number of those originally hired have disappeared and better men have taken their places. Many competent men, who had been driven out of the Brotherhoods for dissolute habits, or from prejudice, and who had at first stood aloof from the trouble, had now come forward and entered the service.

Beginning on the 27th of February with their business almost wholly destroyed, they have used every means in their power, and have left no stone unturned that promised to increase their traffic. In this they have not been unsuccessful, and their business is today probably as good as any other Western road. In their relation to the strikers, they have outwitted them at every point, and have used with fatal effect every weapon that came to their hand. The truth is that the old employes never had a leader, from the 27th of February until the present day; they have been under the orders and at the beck and call of this committee and that committee, and have trusted to this chairman and that chief until they were bewildered, and finally lost. The "Ides of March" was as fatal to them as to Cæsar. When the first boycott was lifted, their defeat was absolute and certain; as an evidence of that the action of the self-constituted Advisory Board, in sending road engineers into the yards in Chicago to take the switch engines given up by their brothers at the second boycott, the last of March, should have been deemed ample and sufficient.

Any strike, by any body of men, conducted as this one was, would have the same ignominious ending. When a class of men are forced into a strike, and their places are filled by men who are allowed to retain them; when the business interests, interrupted by the strike, are permitted to be resumed, does not such a condition plainly indicate failure? There should be no more great railroad strikes until men, other than those immediately interested, are ready and willing to win them.

AT THE CONVENTIONS.

At the Firemen's Convention, the promised plan of federation was put forward. Before the firemen jadourned, the switchmen had met in Convention.

They received and endorsed the plan outlined by the firemen, and appointed a committee of the Grand Officers to act with the engineers and firemen in putting it into execution. Contrary to the expectations of the firemen and switchmen, the engineers at their Convention failed to ratify the move toward federation, and had nothing ready to offer in its stead. They did, however, pass a resolution favoring "some means of bringing the organizations closer together." This action of the engineers was generally understood as a desire upon their part to drop the federation scheme entirely, and much ill feeling has in consequence resulted. The striking switchmen naturally felt that the sacrifice made by them had failed to bear fruit, and that the Brotherhood had not redeemed their pledges—nay, more, that they had fallen back into their old position of "refraining from all entangling alliances" and ignoring the other organizations.

Affairs remained in this unsatisfactory condition until the latter part of November. In the meantime, many of the strikers, engineers, firemen and switchmen sought and obtained work on other roads, the Chicago, Santa Fe & California gaining the most of them.

ANOTHER COMMITTEE.

At the Engineers' Convention, a committee of nine had been appointed, with A. R. Cavener as chairman, to handle the remains of the "Q" strike. Hoge was retired, or rather had resigned, and the payments to the men were now made through the local divisions of the Brotherhood. Up to November 25, nothing had been heard of the committee of nine, and it was not known that they were making any efforts to assist the strikers. It was understood that this committee had been given all the power in the Brotherhood, even to the boycott, if necessary to win the strike.

CUTTING OFF THE SWITCHMEN.

November 25, letters were received by the chairman of each local body of strikers, from Cleveland, signed by P. M. Arthur and the Finance Committee of the Brotherhood of Locomotive Engineers.

These letters were to the effect, that after the October payment had been made, the switchmen were to be stricken from the payrolls; that the late Convention had made no provision for the further payment of these men.

It will be remembered that prior to the switchmen engaging in this strike, an agreement had been made with them that as long as the strike lasted they were to be paid the same wages that were paid to the engineers. A written contract was entered into, a copy of which is now in possession of James L. Monoghan. During the different phases of the strike this agreement was frequently mentioned by prominent members of the Brotherhoods, and acknowledged by the Chiefs.

At the same time the switchmen were cut off from assistance, the pay of the engineers was raised from $40 to $50 per month. This increase of $10 would have been ample to pay the switchmen.

Protests were sent to Cleveland from all over the

"Q" system. The following is the text in full of the Chicago letter, together with the signatures of engineers, firemen and switchmen :

CHICAGO, ILL., NOV. 24, 1888.
HEADQUARTERS C., B. & Q, STRIKERS.—CURRAN'S HALL.
To Messrs. P. M. Arthur, T. S. Ingraham, H. C. Hayes:

DEAR SIRS: In receipt of yours of the 22d, we must say that a more sad turn or blow has not struck this body since the beginning of the strike as the decision of that letter. Have we solicited the friendly hand of our fellow switchmen the past eight months, have we sustained brotherly feeling and fought the common enemy all summer hand in hand, only to throw our participants broadcast over the land after proving themselves loyal to us and men of their word? Do we have to bring disgrace upon ourselves, by being connected with such unmanly actions, and involve thereby bitter antagonistic feelings in the future? We engineers went out with grievances, where the switchmen had none, but sympathy only; would it not be more justice to cut us off and pay these men for their manly actions?

After the return of the regular delegates from the Convention, information was communicated to us of their firm understanding that the treatment of the engineers and switchmen would be the same in the future as in the past.

In regard to dividing our $40 per month with the switchmen in the future, we can only refer to figures; about thirty to thirty-one engineers against sixty-five switchmen [in Chicago—AUTHOR], both parties in debt more or less for the necessaries of life for the eight months, winter at hand, and our men badly in need. Some provision must be made! How in the name of God can we share with others, having scarcely enough for ourselves?

The future prosperity of our Order undoubtedly depends upon the just action taken in this C., B. & Q. struggle. How can we expect to gain and retain the kindly feeling of members of other organizations relative to us in railway service by practicing acts of injustice and partiality in our own midst? Look at the switchmen at this point. When employed, their salary ranges from $75 to $90 per month. They have stepped down for principle's sake, and not for the $40 per month, barely sufficient at this point to keep soul and body together. Now, at this great Convention it has been overlooked to provide for these men who fought the battle according to instructions.

Only a portion of the men being thought of, and the balance of them—those who sacrificed all for principle and friendship—have been thrown out into the world without any previous notice whatever. Here we are today to fight our own battle. Rather than being sacrificed and deserted in this style, we will accept previous favorable offers at Chicago, saving at least this point, although at the sad experience of broken promises.

Indeed, sad it is for men to fight honorably, and with whole soul, only to find out, after losing all, that they are cut off from ammunition! Now then, left without ammunition, what is left for the soldier to do—surrender or be cut down?

Our course in this depends on speedy action, and we therefore demand immediate answer from your Grand Lodge, stating decidedly the future treatment. Shall it continue as before, or shall it be cut off? As our men are radical, we ask you to answer by telegraph, up to 2 P. M.. Monday, November 26, "Yes" or "No." If no answer is received up to this time it will be considered by this body a negative answer, and copies of this will be sent to all subordinate divisions and lodges of the Big Four organizations.　Yours fraternally,

[Signed]　T. J. TIERNEY,　　M. SHIELDS,
　　　　　　M. T. MAHONEY,　JOHN A. HIENISH,
　　　　　　J. RYAN,　　　　DAVID BAIN,
　　　　　　　Engineers.　　　　Switchmen.

The answer came by mail, and reads as follows:

OFFICE OF THE GRAND DIVISION
BROTHERHOOD OF LOCOMOTIVE ENGINEERS,
CLEVELAND, Nov. 26, 1888.

M. T. Mahoney:

DEAR SIR AND BROTHER: Yours of the 24th at hand, and in reply thereto we sent a check Saturday, to pay the engineers and switchmen alike for October. After that time we can pay nothing for the switchmen. You seem to think that the power is vested in the Grand Officers to levy assessments for the support of the switchmen; but such is not the case.

We can only act as directed by the Convention. The Convention directed that an assessment be levied for the support of the engineers at $50 per month, and that is as far as we can act.

Yours fraternally,

[Signed]   T. S. INGRAHAM, F. G. A. E.

Previous to these letters, the Chairman of the switchmen had written to Cleveland to make inquiry about the October pay. The answer to his letter is also herewith given:

CLEVELAND, O., Nov., 22, 1888.

J. A. Hienish, Esq.:

In reply to yours of 18th, I can only say that, although the Grand Chief was particular to call attention to the fact that no provision was made for October payroll, no steps were taken to supply that want, and all that we can do is to forward the amounts as fast as money comes in on donations, which is very slow, and with October payroll all payments to switchmen and brakemen will cease, as the further assessment was levied to pay engineers only. We have, however, advised the engineers to share what they receive with the switchmen.

Whether or not they will do it, they can answer. We shall send a draft today to pay the men at Chicago, both engineers and switchmen for October, and to other points as fast as we can get the money, which is the best we can do.

Yours truly,

[Signed]   T. S. INGRAHAM, F. G. A. E.

Letters were sent by the strikers to all the Brotherhood Divisions throughout the western country, notifying them of the arbitrary action of the officers and telling them the condition of the men.

No word had been received from Chairman Cavener or his committee of nine until after the 9th of December, when the switchmen of Chicago declared the strike off, as far as concerned themselves. This action was taken with the consent and advice of the Grand Master of the Association, and letters were sent to the switchmen along the line of road, advising them to take the same action and make any terms that they were able to make with the company.

The striking engineers and firemen at Chicago also advised this course and even offered to unite with the switchmen in following it out.

The switchmen along the line, acting on the advice of the Brotherhood men, refused to recognize the strike as off, and remained with the engineers, but without aid from the Brotherhood, as seen from the letters herewith given.

December 11, Mr. Cavener arrived in Chicago, and on the 28th of December representatives of the Brotherhood from west of the Missouri river assembled in Chicago to the number of two hundred. They were called together by Mr. Cavener to take final action on the strike.

From the 28th day of December to the 4th day of January, the daily papers were full of sensational rumors of boycotts, but no such action was contemplated by the Brotherhoods.

Below is given the full report of the settlement, issued from the Grand Lodge of the Switchmen's Mutual Aid Association.

OFFICE OF THE GRAND LODGE. SWITCHMEN'S MUTUAL AID ASSOCIATION OF NORTH AMERICA.

CHICAGO, ILL., Jan. 10, 1889.

To All Subordinate Lodges:

SIRS AND BROTHERS: At the late Convention of the Brotherhood of Locomotive Engineers, held at Richmond, Va , a Committee of nine was appointed to examine into the

condition of the strike on the C., B. & Q. Railroad, and devise
ways and means whereby it might be brought to a close.   The
Committee was composed of the following named gentlemen:
A. R. Cavener, A. W. Perley, T. Hollinrake, Thos. Humphreys,
A. Le May, A. W. Logan, Edward Kent, Wm. C. Hayes and T.
P. Bellows.   After the Committee had made a thorough investigation, they requested the Brotherhood of Locomotive
Firemen to appoint a Committee to act in conjunction with
with them, and Grand Master Sargent appointed L. Mooney
and S. W. Dixon as such Committee.   This Joint Committee, in their report to the two Brotherhoods, say: An
interview with the officials of the C., B. & Q. company was
solicited and granted.   Other interviews followed, in which
the strike, in all its details was discussed, with a thorough ap-
preciation of the gravity and importance of the situation.
The Committee sought by all the means at its command to
secure a settlement that would be of the largest possible advantage to the strikers.   Every point was brought out and
thoroughly discussed, and after a careful, patient and ex-
haustive review of the situation, a settlement was effected which
met with the unanimous approval of the Joint Committee.

Preliminary to our report of the settlement, we desire
to introduce the following documents, which are self-explan-
atory:

CHICAGO, Jan. 4, 1889.

Mr. E. P. Ripley, General Manager, Chicago:

DEAR SIR: The enclosed is a copy of the communication which I was directed to give to the Committee of the
Brotherhood of Locomotive Engineers and Firemen, who
have been in conference with us today, which was accepted
by them, and they have declared the strike settled.

It is important that no question should arise as to the
good faith of the company, and it is our desire and intention
that there should be no opportunity for such question.

As to the meaning of the word "available," I desire to
say that when it becomes necessary to employ men outside of
those now in the service, care must be taken to consider all
the qualifications that go to make up availability, including
experience and familiarity with our surroundings and rules.
In short, that the very best men are to be selected, regardless
of personal relations or prejudices for or against any men or
class of men.

It should be further fully understood that the company
does not desire to pursue those who have been guilty of improper conduct during the late strike, and while such men

cannot be re-employed, and while we cannot give letters to them, no officer or employe should continue the animosities of the conflict after it is over, or interfere to prevent the employment of such men elsewhere.   Yours truly,

HENRY B. STONE.

Similar letters will be sent to all the officers in charge of our different properties, and by them transmitted to their operating officers.   H. B. STONE.

WESTERN UNION TELEGRAPH COMPANY.

BOSTON, Jan. 3, 1889.

To Henry B. Stone, Vice President C., B. & Q. Ry., Chicago:

I did not telegraph yesterday, as you requested, because it seemed important under the circumstances, and since we have been asked by the engineers to say what our position is, that it should be done with the authority of the whole Executive Committee. The Committee is now in session, and I am authorized and instructed to send you the following:

"The company will not follow up, black list, or in any manner attempt to proscribe those who were concerned in the strike, but, on the contrary, will cheerfully give to all who have not been guilty of violence, or other improper conduct, letters of introduction, showing their record in our service, and will, in all proper ways, assist them in finding employment.

"The first duty of the management is to those who are in the company's employ, and we must remember, and protect their interests by promotions, and by every other means in our power. Beyond this, if it should become necessary to go outside of the service for men in any capacity, it is our intention to select the best men available, and in making selections, not to exclude those who were engaged in the strike of February 27, if they are the best men available, and provided they have not since been guilty of violence and other improper conduct."

You are authorized to give a copy of this message to the engineers who called upon you.

[Signed]   C. E. PERKINS.

CHICAGO, Jan. 4, 1889.

Mr. A. R. Cavener, Chairman Committee Brotherhood Locomotive Engineers:

DEAR SIR: The above is a copy of a telegram received yesterday from Mr. Perkins, our President, and which, in accordance with his instructions, I have submitted to you, and which has been fully discussed with you and your Committee.

Yours truly,   HENRY B. STONE.

CHICAGO, Jan. 4, 1889.

Mr. Henry B. Stone, Second Vice President:

DEAR SIR: We, the undersigned Committee, in behalf of our respective organizations—Brotherhood of Locomotive Engineers and Brotherhood of Locomotive Firemen —and as representatives of the ex-employes of the Burlington system, who left the services of said company February 27, 1888, or later, on account of the strike, approve of the foregoing agreement, and hereby declare the strike of the said ex-employes as settled.

Yours truly,

ALEX. R. CAVENER,	WM. C. HAYES,
A. W. PERLEY,	A. W. LOGAN,
T. HOLLINRAKE,	EDW. KENT,
THOS. HUMPHREYS,	T. P. BELLOWS,
A. LE MAY,	S. W. DIXON,
	L. MOONEY.

The Joint Committee submitted their report to the Grand Officers of the B. of L. E. and B. of L. F., and the settlement "met with their entire and unqualified approval." The Grand Officers, therefore, issued a circular to their respective Divisions and Lodges, under date of January 7, 1889, in which they say "The strike of the Brotherhood of Locomotive Engineers and Brotherhood of Locomotive Firemen on the C., B. & Q. railway system, inaugurated February 27, 1888, is hereby officially declared at an end, and the striking employes are now at liberty to make applications for situations on said system."

The purpose of this circular is to advise the striking switchmen who desire to be re-employed, to file their applications at their respective Division headquarters, on or before February 1, 1889. This advice is given at the request of the officials of the company. Applications filed after February 1 will not be considered.

The settlement may not be all that might be expected or desired, but it seems to be the best that could be secured under the condition of things, and I hope it will be received in good faith, and that all hostility will cease.

In closing, I urge upon switchmen, members of our Association, to exert their influence in securing situations for the ex-employes of the C., B. & Q. system.

Yours fraternally, FRANK SWEENEY,
Grand Master S. M. A. A. of N. A.

The letters herein printed are given without comment, further than to say that as they seem to have some bearing on the settlement, they were evidently intended for that purpose.

The business of the Burlington, as with the other western roads at this time, is but little over half its usual volume. No switchmen, engineers or firemen returned to the employ of that company during January. Advices from along the entire system indicate the same condition of affairs at the present date, February 8, 1889. The new men, laid off on account of dull business, still remain on hand, and as business increases they will return to work, and not until their ranks are exhausted will there be any vacancies for the old men. The probabilities are, that several months will elapse before any of the strikers will be needed by the Burlington road.

The following letters having been made public by the Grand Officers of the firemen, through the medium of their magazine, we violate no confidence in giving them publicity here. We particularly desire to print them, from the fact that they indicate a condition of affairs in relation to the settlement that should be made known to the general public. The letters and comments are from the February, 1889, number of the Firemen's Magazine.

"The B. of L. E., at its Richmond Convention, not only declined to repeal laws, the enactment of which was an indignity of such unquestioned insolence, that 'a wayfaring man though a fool' need not err in comprehending the outrage, but in its deliberations relating to ending the C., B. & Q. strike, it concluded to ignore the B. of L. F. entirely, as if the Order had no interests at stake and was unworthy of notice. In proof of this we introduce here an extract of a letter from P. M. Arthur, Grand Chief, dated November 5, 1888, which is conclusive :

" The Convention also decided to appoint a Committee of nine, with Bro. Alex. Cavener as chairman, to determine when the strike *shall end* on the C., B. & Q. Bro. Cavener will first go over that system, and see how the situation is, and address the men at the different places on the line, in view of a *settlement*. After which he will *convene his Committee* and they are to *decide when the trouble shall end*, and *no one but themselves is to know the result until they report to the Grand Officers.*

"We have italicised certain expressions in Grand Chief Arthur's letter to Grand Master Sargent, to enable our readers to see how effectually the B. of L. F. was squelched, left out in the cold, disregarded and tabooed by the B. of L. E. in the 'settlement' of the strike.

"In reply to Grand Chief Arthur's letter of November 5, we here introduce extracts from Grand Master Sargent's letter of November 7 :

P. M. Arthur, Esq. :

DEAR SIR AND BROTHER: I am in receipt of your communication of November 5, written by S. G. E. Bro. Everett, and I have noted its contents carefully and I must acknowledge that I am disappointed in the action taken at Richmond on the question of federation.

Referring to the strike, I had hoped that your Convention would end it, believing as I do that it is a useless waste of time and money to continue it any longer. We are already feeling the strain ourselves; my mail is continually filled with communications coming from the officers of the Subordinate Lodges, appealing to me in behalf of their members to excuse them from paying the heavy assessments which we

8

have been compelled to levy. Others are prepared to surrender their charters, and the situation is anything but agreeable to me. There can be no change, however, until such time as the strike is declared off. And we will be compelled to contribute to the support of these men for a long time after, as many of them will be without situations. Whatever may be the decision of the Committee which you have appointed, I hope that they will bear in mind that the Brotherhood of Locomotive Firemen are just as much interested in this strike as is the Brotherhood of Locomotive Engineers and that they will also consider this claim, that the members of the Brotherhood of Firemen are not all wealthy men.

"In reply to Grand Master Sargent's letter of the 7th, Grand Chief Arthur writes as follows, under date of November 9:

In regard to the strike we are deeply sensible of the circumstances by which you are surrounded, and nothing could have been further from our thought than to ignore you or your Brotherhood, but in view of the fact that your Convention adjourned without action touching that matter, and as you had expressed a hope that our Convention should declare it off, it was deemed wise to take steps to fix a time to end it without giving any aid or comfort to the company.

This is what was kept in view and the welfare of the firemen in it was as much an object as was that of the engineers, and when the Committee reports you will be fully informed of the course decided upon.

"We are not disposed to indulge in severity of language in criticising Grand Chief Arthur's letter to Grand Master Sargent, of November 9. It is easily seen that Mr. Arthur was not only 'deeply sensible' of the circumstances which 'surrounded' the B. of L. F., but was quite as 'deeply sensible' that the circumstances 'which surrounded' the B. of L. E. were of character which he found it exceedingly difficult to explain. When the B. of L. E. deliberately 'ignored' the B. of

L. F., giving it a direct slap in the face in a matter in
which the interests of its members were vitally involved, the declarations of the Grand Chief 'that
nothing could have been further from our thoughts
than to ignore you or your Brotherhood,' the very
climax of irony is reached.   Look at it; here were
two great Brotherhoods engaged in a life and death
struggle with a powerful corporation.   It had cost
them hundreds of thousands of dollars.   Firemen, with
a fidelity born of heroism worthy of monuments of
marble, had stood by the engineers until they were
impoverished.   At this supreme juncture, the B. of
L. E. concludes to take steps to terminate the strike.
Does it consider the interests, the rights, the sacrifices
of the B. of L. F.?   No, not in the least.   There is
no word, no sign of recognition.   On the contrary the
action of the B. of L. E. is that of the most offensive
ostracism.   There is not so much as a squint at co-
operation or federation.   The gush and slush about the
'twin Brotherhoods' disappears, and yet Grand Chief
Arthur declares, as if he expected his assertion would
be accepted as true. that in the appointment of a Committee of nine, clothed with full power to settle the
strike, in which no reference was made to the B. of L.
F. or to its interests, 'nothing could have been further
from our thought than to ignore' the B. of L. F.   It
is sufficient to say that the declaration of Grand Chief
Arthur was not accepted as conclusive.   It is neither
an apology nor an explanation.   Indeed, it only serves
to emphasize the fact that the B. of L. E. deliberately
and purposely ignored the B. of L. F.

"Proceeding with the history, it will be seen that Mr. Alexander R. Cavener, Chairman of the Committee of nine engineers, proceeded to carry out his instructions. He went over the roads of the 'Q' system, he held meetings and obtained information. He assembled his Committee of engineers and made his reports. The conclusion was to declare the strike at an end. In all of this no fireman had been consulted —no attention paid to the B. of L. F. officers or men. There had been neither co-operation nor federation— no allusion to the 'twin (?) Brotherhoods.'

"At this juncture, Mr. Alexander R. Cavener, Chairman of the Committee of nine, bethought himself of the fact that there was such a Brotherhood as the B. of L. F. The B. of L. E. had not authorized him to indulge such a thought, but he did remember it and sent the following telegram:

CHICAGO, Dec. 27, 1888.
Sargent and Debs:

Can you select a Committee of your Order to act in conjunction with our Committee? Meet us at Commercial Hotel morning of December 29.

[Signed]   ALEX. R. CAVENER.

" This was the first intimation the B. of L. F. had that the B. of L. E., or the Committee of nine, recognized that the B. of L. F. had any interest whatever in the 'Q' strike, or in the settlement of the strike. Grand Master Sargent was not in Terre Haute when the message was received, and Grand Secretary and Treasurer Debs, of the B. of L. F., replied as follows:

TERRE HAUTE, IND., Dec. 27, 1888.

Grand Master Sargent is expected home from the East this evening, and your message will be referred to him on his arrival. For myself I do not favor the appointment of a Committee such as you suggest at this time. The invitation for joint procedure comes too late in the day. I have no doubt our regular Committee representing the C. B. & Q., now at Chicago, will be amply able to look after our interests.

E. V. DEBS.

"Upon the arrival of Grand Master Sargent the following message was sent to Chairman Cavener, at Chicago:

TERRE HAUTE, IND., Dec. 29, 1888.

A. R. Cavener, Commercial Hotel, Chicago, Ill.:

Referring to your telegram we have to say, that in our opinion we should have been given an opportunity of being represented in the tour of inspection of the "Q" system. We are in the habit of acting for ourselves in such matters, and hence we are not disposed at this late hour to join in the "amen" to what has been done. If we were not capable of doing our part from the beginning we are not willing to join issues now. We respectfully decline to appoint any Committee for the purpose suggested in your telegram.

[Signed]   F. P. SARGENT, Grand Master.
         E. V. DEBS, Grand Sec. & Treas.

"The refusal of the B. of L. F. to appoint a Committee to act with the engineers' Committee was adversely criticised, and resulted in sending to Terre Haute a Committee of two, Bro. R. H. Lacy, Chairman of the C., B. & Q. Committee, having charge of strike affairs, and Bro. George Godding. These men visited Terre Haute, and, acting under advice, represented to Grand Master Sargent that it was important that a Committee should be appointed to represent the firemen on the Committee of engineers.

"Grand Master Sargent thereupon transmitted to Grand Chief Arthur the following message:

TERRE HAUTE, IND., Jan. 2, 1889.

P. M. Arthur, Cleveland, Ohio:

I have been requested by A. R. Cavener, Chairman of Committee at Chicago, to appoint a Committee of firemen to act with them in the matter now before them. Will you inform me if he has the authority to do this, and if you approve of the same as the Executive of the Order? Has this Committee full power to act regardless of you? Answer at my expense.

[Signed]   F. P. SARGENT, Grand Master.

"In response to the foregoing, the following reply was received from Grand Chief Arthur:

CLEVELAND, O., Jan. 2, 1889.

Frank P. Sargent:

Would advise you to grant Cavener's request in the interest of peace and harmony. He has not complied with my instructions, but I waive all in favor of having an end put to the strike.

P. M. ARTHUR.

"Upon receipt of this message, Grand Master Sargent appointed Bros. S. W. Dixon, of Baraboo, Wis., and L. Mooney, of St. Joe, Mo., a Committee to represent the B. of L. F.'s interests, as set forth in the following communication addressed to Chairman Cavener of the B. of L. E. Committee under date of January 2:

GRAND LODGE
BROTHERHOOD OF LOCOMOTIVE FIREMEN.
TERRE HAUTE, IND., Jan. 2, 1889.

A. R. Cavener, Esq., and members of the Committee representing the Brotherhood of Locomotive Engineers and the interests of the C., B. & Q. engineers engaged in the present strike:

GENTLEMEN AND BROTHERS: It is not necessary for me to introduce myself to you honorable gentlemen, as I am, no doubt, known to you both officially and socially, and I will proceed to place before you certain facts, and at the same time explain to you the reason of my forwarding the message to Bro. Cavener, Chairman of your Committee, signed jointly by Bro. Debs and myself, in reply to a request made by Bro. Cavener for us to appoint a Committee representing the firemen to go with you before the officials of the Burlington system. I desire to trespass upon your valuable time long enough to call your attention to the original compact entered into between the engineers and firemen in the beginning of this eventful strike. It was understood that in all our dealings both as Committees and as executive officers among ourselves, or when before the officers of the company, that we should act together. I am not disposed at this time to pass any criticism whatever upon the action of the Brotherhood of Locomotive Engineers or upon any of its executive officers; I simply wish to call attention to this matter in a fair and unbiased light.

When our Convention convened at Atlanta, the situation of the Brotherhood was not of an encouraging nature; we were incumbered with debt; we knew that we could not as a body, take any action in the matter of the strike, except to provide means for the maintenance of the men engaged therein, until such time as the Convention of your honorable body had convened and decided upon what they believed to be the best course to pursue. We provided means for the further sustenance of our men and awaited the action of your body. Being honored with an invitation to be present in Richmond as a guest of your Brotherhood, I was able to meet with many of the prominent members, together with the Grand Officers, and I presented, when the opportunity offered, my exact position as an Executive Official, stating, that we, as an organization, were willing, at all times to do anything that was honorable toward bringing about a satisfactory settlement of the difficulty. I was assured that some action would be taken whereby some means would be devised which would lead to the ending of the strike. I returned home, and shortly after the termination of your Convention, I received an official communication from Grand Chief Arthur, in which he informed me that a Committee of nine had been appointed with Bro. Alex. R. Cavener as Chairman, to determine when the strike should end on the C., B. & Q.; that Bro. Cavener should

first go over the system and see what the situation was, and
address the men at different places along the line in view of
a settlement; after which he would convene the Committee,
and they were to decide when the trouble should end, and
no one but themselves was to know the result until after re-
porting to the Grand Office. I immediately wrote a letter to
Grand Chief Arthur, in which I expressed a feeling of dissatisfaction on account of the firemen not being requested to
to appoint members of the organization to represent them;
I believed that if there was a representative of the engineers
organization going over the system that there should also be
a representative of the firemen accompanying him. I may
have been wrong in my view, still I have seen nothing yet to
change my opinion. In reply to my letter to Grand Chief
Arthur, he stated that it was not the intention to ignore us in
any manner, but as I had expressed the hope that his Convention would devise the means of ending the strike, it was
deemed wise to take steps and fix a time to end it without
giving any aid or comfort to the company. He further stated
that the firemen and their welfare were kept in view, and that
when the Committee made its report that I would be fully informed of the course decided upon, no intimation being made,
however, that I was at liberty to appoint any firemen to go in
conjunction with the Committee of engineers. While the communication did not just meet my views, I said to my associate,
" We will await the report of this Committee." A few days
after I visited Cleveland and had a conversation with Grand
Chief Arthur, in which I again broached this matter, and was
again informed by him that it was no intention on the part of
the Convention to ignore the firemen and that our interests
were considered equally with theirs. He furthermore informed
me regarding the authority delegated to the Committee, and
led me to believe that all you could do was simply to assem-
ble, receive the report of Bro. Cavener, and then recommend
what further action should be taken by the Grand Officers
when we should convene as Grand Officers and decide the
issue. A few days after this I was present in the city of St.
Paul, and had a pleasant interview with Bro. Hayes, who is, I
believe, a member of your Committee. I expressed to Bro.
Hayes my opinion, and I desire to say I found him exceedingly
courteous, and he coincided with my views, saying it was all

due to an oversight and that he would communicate with Grand Chief Arthur on the subject. I stated to Bro. Hayes that if Grand Chief Arthur requested of me the appointment of a Committee, I would gladly do so; nothing more was heard of the matter. I was receiving communications daily from all sections of the country, asking why the firemen were not represented on this Committee; such communications I answered in as honorable a manner as I knew how, placing no censure upon any one and saying nothing that would in any manner, lead intelligent men to think we had any desire to antagonize.

In my absence from the city Bro. Debs received a telegram from Bro. Cavener, requesting us to appoint a committee. Bro. Debs answered the message, expressing his sentiments, not for the purpose of creating ill-feeling, but simply to place us and our Order before the Committee in an honorable light. Upon my return the message was submitted to me, and in view of the fact that throughout this entire strike we have acted jointly, believing that we should have been requested to make appointments on that Committee of engineers, and in view of the further fact that at the time of learning officially of the action of the Committee, I wrote to Grand Chief Arthur, calling his attention to my feelings and afterward in my conversation with Brother Hayes, in which I gave him to understand that if Grand Chief Arthur would request of me the appointing of a Committee that I would gladly do so. I believed, as did Bro. Debs, that it was entirely wrong to ask us to send a Committee to go before the officers of the company after the Committee's work in a large measure had been accomplished. When I say "Committee's work" I refer to the Chairman, who had been over the system interviewing men and observing the situation while we were not represented nor even requested to be; and for this reason our message was sent. This morning a Committee of two of the General Committee representing the firemen on the C., B. & Q. R. R. presented the position you occupy and authority delegated to you by your Grand Body. After a careful consideration of the matter and a desire to bring about an amicable settlement of the present difficulty, create harmony and good will between all labor organizations, especially our co-workers, the engineers, we have wired the following message to Grand

Chief Arthur: "I have been requested by A. R. Cavener, Chairman of Committee at Chicago, to appoint a committee of firemen to act with others in the matter now before them. Will you inform me if he has the authority to do this and if you approve of the same as the Executive of the Order? Has this Committee full power to act regardless of you? Answer at my expense."

Considering the correspondence and conversation we have had on this subject with Grand Chief Arthur, it is no more than right that he should, as an executive of the organization he represents, endorse the appointing of a Committee representing the firemen, to take part in these deliberations. Upon receiving his reply, if he endorses your request, I shall immediately instruct two members of our Order, who are intelligent, capable and somewhat familiar with the situation, to report to you at once. I can assure you that whatever you decide upon doing, these representatives will acquiesce in so long as it is to the interests of the organizations involved.

I am sorry that there should be any misunderstanding on account of this matter, but I think time will demonstrate to intelligent, thinking minds that the position taken by the Grand Officers of the B. of L. F. has been an honorable one, and all we ask is that consideration which all honest men are entitled to. We may differ in opinion, but that we have a right to do, and when it comes to a matter of such grave importance as the one that now presents itself for our consideration, we should set aside all personal feelings and act to the best interests of those we represent.

I can assure you, gentlemen, that you have the best wishes of the Grand Officers of the Brotherhood of Locomotive Firemen, and we only trust that through your deliberations may come such good results as will redound in honor to yourselves as well as to the organization which you represent.   Yours fraternally,

                         F. P. SARGENT.

"In this connection it becomes necessary to state that among other things charged in support of the allegations that the B. of L. F. is responsible for the failure of the strike, is a letter written by Grand

Master Sargent in reply to a letter received from Bro. J. E. Kline, of Plattsmouth, Neb. As special efforts have been made to misrepresent Grand Master Sargent in the matter, we here give the full text of the correspondence :

PLATTSMOUTH, NEB., Dec. 6, 1888.

F. P. Sargent, Esq., Grand Master :

DEAR SIR AND BROTHER : Yours of recent date to Bro. Zinn was referred to me, and I was requested to ask for information. Since you cannot assure us our support after November, can you give us any encouragement in regard to the Committee of nine, with Cavener at the head, which was appointed at the late Engineers' Convention? We have been notified that they would put on the boycott, which I think is the only means to win this fight. I am very much afraid that this strike is lost, and that we (the men on the Q.) are sacrificed. I have been a Brotherhood fireman about two years, and have done everything in my power to promote the Order, and I have always thought that nothing could break our organization, but I am afraid if this strike is lost, that we fall beneath the heels of capital; yet I am satisfied that some move can be made by our Order to crush the C., B. & Q. into submission. Now, in regard to some of the strikers refusing employment on other roads, preferring to lay idle on the forty ($40) dollars paid us for so doing, I think is false, and I am satisfied I can convince your informant. In the first place, well do you know that there are many roads that want men, but refuse to employ C., B. & Q. strikers, until the strike is declared off. Furthermore, we have men working on all the roads in the country that will employ strikers. I am sorry that those men who are being expelled for non-payment, cannot see that it is to their benefit to sacrifice a few dollars per month, while we who are in the fight sacrifice on an average of thirty-five ($35) dollars per month. I would to God that those men have their wages cut down one-half in the next twenty-four hours. In conclusion, I ask you your *candid opinion in regard to the boycott.* Please let me hear from you at once.

Sincerely yours, JNO. E. KLINE.

GRAND LODGE
BROTHERHOOD OF LOCOMOTIVE FIREMEN,
TERRE HAUTE, IND., Dec. 14, 1888.

DEAR SIR AND BROTHER: Your favor of December 6 came to hand during my absence from the city, which accounts for a delayed answer. I cannot give you any information of the action of the Committee appointed by the engineers in their Convention, other than what I received from Grand Chief Arthur and one member of the Committee. I have heard that it was the intention of the Committee to end the strike; but I can say to you honestly and candidly, that so far as a boycott is concerned it is simply nonsense to talk about it. Any sane man who will carefully consider the present situation of the C . B. & Q., and the condition of our organization, would see the folly of our contemplating such a step. The day for boycott has long gone by; there was a time when it could have been put into effect, and something accomplished by it, had there been any disposition on the part of a large number of men to maintain it, but any man who was a witness of the situation at Chicago, during the time of the boycott, would see the folly of talking about one in this instance; and I must say to you very firmly and honestly, that the Brotherhood of Locomotive Firemen, as an organization, will have nothing whatever to do with a boycott, no matter what Mr. Cavener's statements may be. I am waiting for the report of this Committee which has been appointed by the engineers. When their report comes in, if they have no way of ending the strike, I will find a way of getting the Brotherhood of Locomotive Firemen out of it, and I will go to work and endeavor to find employment for our members who are not able to find it themselves. It is a very good idea to go to work and preach federation and all these different doctrines, and then, when the time comes to act upon them, repudiate them. There is no man who appreciates the manly stand of the C., B. & Q. firemen more than I, and there is no one in a better position to see the condition of the organization than I am. I am speaking for no effect other than to express my honest opinion. The time has come when this strike must end and the men must look for employment, and the quicker this is done the better it will be for all concerned. There are those in our Order who are not earning $40 per month and whose wages are far below the

wages paid on the Western roads. These men have paid their
last dollar and they are in want; their families must have
clothes, they must have fuel to keep them warm; and I can
tell you as a friend and brother that I do not propose to drive
such men out of the organization after having done what they
could to maintain the strike. As soon as the strike is off we
will devote our time and attention to finding employment for
such men as desire to make application to the Grand Officers.

Let the consequences be what they will, we have decided
upon the stand we shall take, and I shall take it as an official
of the Order. The engineers in their Convention were informed of my opinion, as was Mr. Cavener, and it seems to me
that when their Committee was appointed, it would have been
nothing more than proper courtesy to have requested one of
our members to act with them. This they did not do. They
say it was an oversight, but it does not change my opinion as
to their duty. I have learned through a member of the Committee of what their action will be; and I desire to say to you
as a brother, with the best feelings towards you and other
members of your Lodge and all strikers, that the advice we
gave you in our last communication was for your best interests
as well as to the interests of every member in the country.
The men who preach boycott had better be engaged in bringing about federation of the different organizations, so that
they may act in harmony one with another. Better be men
and acknowledge the strike lost, look for work and get themselves in a position to fight again when we are called upon to
do so.

I trust you will receive this communication in the spirit
in which it is written, as I desire to be honest with you and
to give you what I believe the best advice that I possibly can.
and, mark my words, the day will come when you will say
that I was right. It may be when I am officially dead, but I
know what the final result will be. I have the best of feeling
for the engineers on the Burlington system, they have done
their duty and done it manfully; and had they the support
which they ought to have had, the result of the strike would
have been very different.

Trusting that the Brothers have decided to take the
advice of one who is their friend, and if they desire assistance

in the way of positions and situations that they will apply for them, and wishing you all success, I remain,

Yours fraternally,

FRANK P. SARGENT, G. M.

"The particular charge made was that Grand Master Sargent had advised firemen to take the places of engineers. And upon this gratuitous falsehood every conceivable charge has been rung. It will be observed that there is not so much as an intimation of such a thing, nor can any amount of torture of Grand Master Sargent's language make it convey such an idea."